STEALING LIFE

T.A. CHASE

Stealing Life
ISBN # 978-1-78184-640-7
©Copyright T.A. Chase 2013
Cover Art by Artist ©Copyright May 2013
Interior text design by Claire Siemaszkiewicz
Totally Bound Publishing

Published in 2013 by Totally Bound Publishing, Newland House, The Point, Weaver Road, Lincoln, LN6 3QN

The Four Horsemen
Pestilence
War
Famine
Death

The Beasor Chronicles
Gypsies
Tramps

Home
No Going Home
Home of His Own
Wishing for a Home
Leaving Home
Home Sweet Home

Every Shattered Dream
Part One
Part Two
Part Three
Part Four
Part Five

Anthologies:
Unconventional at Best: Ninja Cupcakes
Unconventional in Atlanta: His Last Client

Out of Light into Darkness
From Slavery to Freedom
The Vanguard
Two for One
Where the Devil Dances

STEALING LIFE

Dedication

Rue and Vlatko are damaged men, who together heal each other's wounds. Love can truly be a soothing balm for aching hearts.

Chapter One

Hanging by his arms from a tree waiting for darkness to fall gave Rue a lot of time to contemplate his life. He'd made tons of mistakes in the twenty some years he'd lived, but his biggest had to be catching a ride on the cargo ship. Still, it had been the only option left to him. He'd really needed to leave Way Station Nine before security caught him.

Unfortunately, he was now naked. He rested his forehead against the rough bark and prayed there weren't any ants or insects living in the wood. Insects and his naked body didn't mix. *Damn those guys.* He'd never expected them to abandon him in the clearing, hiding his clothes and leaving his bare ass tied to a tree waiting for some fucking huge animal to come and eat him alive — they'd been graphic about what would happen to him. He'd thought they were just going to drop him in the clearing, and he would make up some explanation as how he came to be there when he was found. He should've known better.

So maybe his biggest mistake hadn't been the cargo ship. It might have been making lewd advances towards the captain. Bad luck for him. The captain was a Castan from the planet Casta, one of those places where gay love was frowned upon to the extent that two men caught touching in any way could be killed. Lucky for Rue, the captain didn't feel like killing him. The captain was into torture, Rue guessed, because waiting until the big animals arrived was driving him insane.

The undergrowth rustled and Rue hugged the tree tighter. Someone had once said only the smart die young, so he'd figured he was destined to live forever. Yet somehow, there'd been a miscommunication with his gods and they'd abandoned him to his gruesome death. A totally unrelated thought popped into his head—the ugly birthmark on his back was really beginning to itch. He wished there was some way he could scratch it, but his arms were fastened to the tree with ropes, and had gone numb, so he couldn't move.

Whatever was in the bushes moved closer. Rue shut his eyes and started praying. "Gods, if you're out there, please save me. I promise, no more stealing or whoring. No more taking advantage of blind beggars and cripples. I'll go to Temple every Holy day."

He was babbling, but hell, the gods should be used to people ignoring them until the person praying needed saving. He thumped his forehead against the tree. Maybe praying now wasn't a good idea. The gods had no reason to help him out. He wasn't exactly a shining example of a good person. He tried to shrug. What did the gods expect? His mother had abandoned him on the streets when he was five. He'd survived any way possible. Maybe it wasn't following the golden road to the Heavens, but he didn't go hungry too often.

The sound of grass and twigs crunching underfoot caught his attention as the creature stalking him stepped into the clearing. This was it. He was going to be ripped to shreds without anyone anywhere mourning his passing. Warm breath brushed over his neck and he bent his head forward, offering his naked neck and hoping for a quick death. The scent filling his nose wasn't that of an animal. It was a strange combination of musk and orange. A finger or claw — he didn't know which — traced the outline of his birthmark.

A crazy urge came over him to beg his soon-to-be killer to scratch his back. He laughed wildly. *The things you think about when you're about to die.* His own breath caught in his chest as the creature moved to stand where Rue could see it, if his eyes were open.

"Open your eyes."

The order came as such a shock that Rue's eyes popped open without a thought from him. Rue was happy he was tied to the tree because he would have fallen over in shock at the sight greeting him.

Vlatko stared at the strange man tied spread-eagled to the oak. He hadn't believed the children when they'd come running into his hut, yelling about the ships and the men. He'd hoped it had been their active imaginations making things up, but he had gone out to investigate anyway.

Amazement had swamped him when he'd stepped into the clearing and seen the man. As Vlatko had walked closer, the man had started praying to his gods. Vlatko knew it was futile to pray to any gods. They were on their own in the universe. That was why he'd chosen to get lost on a small planet as close to the edge of nowhere as he could get.

He traced the red mark on the man's back. He knew it was just a birthmark, but the simple people of this planet were going to freak when they saw it. A stranger with a birthmark in the shape of a firebird tied to their sacred tree would push these people into a frenzy if they found out about it.

The naked man bent his head forward, offering up his body as a sacrifice. Vlatko couldn't help himself. He leaned in and breathed the man's scent. The acidic tang of fear was there, but buried beneath was the arousing smell of man. It had been a long time since he'd let his body react to the male scent. However, there was no one with him in the clearing, so he loosened his control.

His cock swelled and his balls tightened. Lust flowed through him. His breathing came quicker. He fought the urge to lick the exposed neck and taste the helpless man before him. The man laughed and Vlatko could hear the fear in the man's voice. Now wasn't the time to indulge his urges.

He circled around to look at the man's face. The stranger had his eyes scrunched shut. *Probably didn't want to see his killer*, Vlatko thought. He didn't really blame the man. Not everyone was brave enough to face his or her own death.

"Open your eyes."

The stranger's eyes popped open and Vlatko had to muffle his gasp. The man had firebird eyes—strange amber, with gold sparks and orange flames burning in them. Vlatko blinked. The eyes staring back at him were still amber, but there were no longer any orange flames.

"Who are you?"

Vlatko smiled at the nerve of the helpless man to question him. "Tell me your name and then maybe I'll share mine."

"Why should I tell you who I am?" The square chin lifted and those amber eyes glared at him arrogantly.

"It seems to me you're in no position to make demands or ask questions, sir. I'm surprised you lasted this long tied to the firebird's tree. She isn't tolerant of strangers." Vlatko gestured up into the branches, where a large bird sat staring down at them.

"Yet she let you get near enough to kill me."

"She and I have an understanding. She doesn't try to light me on fire and I don't try to kill her." Vlatko pulled his knife. "I haven't killed you yet."

"That's amazing in itself because I don't usually inspire patience in anyone I meet." The man laughed.

Vlatko couldn't tell if the stranger was crazy or just resigned to his fate, whatever it might be. He sliced through the ropes holding the man to the tree. The firebird above them screeched and a cascade of sparks rained down on them.

"We're leaving, you old biddy." Vlatko didn't wait to see if the stranger could stand on his own or not. He leant down and slung the man over his shoulder.

A moment or two of silence covered them as Vlatko made his way out of the clearing. The man chuckled a few minutes later.

"I guess I should introduce myself since you have your hand on a very private part of my anatomy." The man flexed his ass cheeks.

Vlatko realised one of his arms was wrapped around the man's legs and the hand of his other arm rested on the man's tight little ass. He didn't drop it, though. "Sorry. Please do tell me your name. I need to know who to listen for in the news reports."

"I'm Rue, and I'm crushed you think I'd be mentioned at all. I'm very good at what I do." Rue's voice was filled with pride and laughter.

Vlatko slapped the firm flesh under his hand. "I'm Vlatko and *I* recognise a street thief when I see one. Even without the brand on your arm."

"Damn. One mistake and you're branded for life. So what are you going to do with me, Vlatko?" Rue slid his hand over Vlatko's back.

Vlatko tried not to think about how Rue's warm hand felt on his skin. It had been a long time since he'd allowed anyone to touch him.

What was he going to do with the thief? It was a good question, but not one Vlatko could answer at the moment. He still had to get Rue into his house without the villagers getting a glimpse of the man's birthmark. With the kind of ethics a thief had, if he knew how the simple people of this world worshipped the firebird, he'd be ruling the planet within days.

Vlatko pushed open the door to his house, making his way to his bedroom after kicking the door shut. He tossed Rue onto his bed and followed him down, pinning the smaller man to the covers. Vlatko tried to ignore how his cock stiffened and his pulse raced at being so close to Rue. He couldn't be distracted by his attraction.

"So what did you steal to warrant being left on a planet like this?" He wasn't sure he wanted to know the answer.

Rue stared up at Vlatko. His mind tried to focus on the question the man asked him, but his cock was mainly concerned with Vlatko's large muscular body pressing him down into the blankets. Rue shifted a little, trying to act as if he wanted to get away, but he just wanted to rub their groins together.

A moan burst from him as the smooth material of Vlatko's leather pants teased his naked cock. Through half-closed eyes, he saw lust burst into Vlatko's dark gaze. He lifted his head until their mouths were only inches apart.

"Kiss me," he demanded.

Vlatko closed those last few inches, but instead of Rue feeling those thin lips, all he got was a stroke of Vlatko's tongue.

"For being a thief and at the mercy of my will, you're rather demanding. You'll get your kiss, but at my discretion, not your demand."

Vlatko pushed off the bed and stood beside it, staring down at him. Rue had never felt embarrassment like he did now as the man's gaze roved over him. He turned his head away, searching for something to cover himself with. Without a word, Vlatko handed him a shirt.

"Thanks," he mumbled while pulling the fabric over his head. He climbed out of bed and the hem dropped to his knees. He was swimming in fabric. Shit—now he looked like a twelve-year-old, which was *so* sexy. He'd have to find clothes that fitted him soon. There was no way he'd be able to convince Vlatko to fuck him and believe his lies while looking like a kid playing dress-up. Rue scowled up at Vlatko as the man smiled.

"I'll find clothes to fit you later, but first, you haven't answered my question. What did you steal?" Vlatko crossed his thick forearms over his wide chest.

Again Rue's brain tried to short-circuit, but he managed to stay on topic. "I'm hurt. What makes you think I took anything?" He placed his hand on his chest and pouted, trying for his best wounded, innocent expression.

"Besides the brand on your arm, just a hunch. I intercepted a universal be-on-the-look-out from the security detachment at Way Station Nine about a thief matching your description." Vlatko raised an eyebrow. "Want to try that innocent act again?"

"Fuck." Rue searched for a way out. Vlatko stood in front of the hut's door, the only visible escape route. Yet Vlatko had the aura of a soldier about him, so Rue was sure there would be another exit hidden somewhere. "Damn. I didn't think they'd get a BOLO out so soon."

"Don't try to run, Rue. It'll only get you killed." Vlatko relaxed against the door.

Rue was amazed the wood managed to hold up under Vlatko's weight. "So you're going to kill me after all?" He shook his head. "I should have known. I'm trying to make a living, surviving the best I know how, and everyone says I'm a thief."

"I didn't say I'd kill you." Vlatko dropped his arms and hooked his thumbs in his belt, framing the bulge behind his zipper with his fingers.

"Um… If you aren't going to…" Rue's eyes zeroed in on the large hard-on Vlatko was sporting. "Um…kill me, who will?"

"The people living on this planet. It's the birthmark on your back." Vlatko nodded at him, stroking his fingers up and down the front of his pants. "It's a symbol of their most sacred religious icon. The tree you were tied to—they'd kill you under it and let your blood water its roots."

Rue shivered, but he wasn't sure if it was from lust or fear. "I don't know what I took." That was the truth. His client had asked for a certain stone and Rue had made sure he'd grabbed that one.

"So you were just stealing?"

Rue wondered if Vlatko was being sarcastic, but there wasn't any emotion on the big man's face except curiosity.

"It's what I do and I'm good at it, considering I've been doing it since I was five years old." It wasn't bragging when it was the truth.

He'd only been caught once, when he was ten. After the Inter-Universal Military had finished branding him, they'd dumped him back on the streets. He'd got an infection, but hadn't got a clue. Stealing and conning people were all he knew. Until he learnt some other way to eat, he'd keep doing it.

"I was making my way through the crowd at the way station. There was a group of six or seven people standing by the loading dock for a transport to Villaria. They were well-dressed, so I thought I'd relieve them of some of their baubles." He shrugged as he moved closer to Vlatko. Rue licked his lips. He wanted to taste the big man.

Vlatko's black hair was braided into a thousand small, intricate braids with beads, feathers and ribbons entwined amongst them. His skin was a dark brown. It reminded Rue of a leather couch he'd once seen in the living room of a house he'd been robbing. He wondered if Vlatko's skin would be as soft to the touch as the leather had been. Vlatko wore a simple green leather tunic. It was sleeveless and laced up the sides. Tight black leather pants and black military issue boots completed the masculine picture trying to overwhelm Rue's brain.

"The group you ran amok in was from a small outer universe planet called Mitcov." Vlatko didn't stop Rue from coming closer. "Besides money and baubles, one of the things you relieved from them was the key to Mitcov's survival."

"Fuck me. I didn't steal anything like that." He thought back to the pocketful of items he'd taken off them before he'd moved to the next loading dock. He hadn't had time to go through and make sure he'd actually got what his client wanted. Now from what Vlatko was telling him, he'd been successful.

"Yes, you did. You stole the Councillor's Heart, Rue, and they'll stop at nothing to find and kill you." Vlatko grabbed Rue's wrist and yanked him up against his body.

Whoever your client is has screwed you over. The man might be right. That was the last thought running through Rue's mind before it shut down as Vlatko's lips took his without mercy.

Vlatko was sure kissing the beautiful thief wasn't the smartest thing to do, but he didn't believe always doing the smart thing was the best way to live. He could admit to himself that he enjoyed taking risks, and fucking Rue seemed the biggest risk of all.

He picked Rue up, then carried him back to the cot. After tossing Rue down, he gestured for the thief to stay put. Vlatko stripped with quick, efficient movements. The Inter-Universal Military didn't have a rule against sexual encounters among its men, but the soldiers had learnt not to waste time on foreplay. He couldn't keep a grin of pride from his face at the wonder in Rue's eyes.

The thief reached out with those elegant hands to cup Vlatko's balls and wrap his cock in a fist. They were pickpocket hands and Rue was showing him why the man was considered one of the best thieves in the universe.

Rue moved his fingers in a soft dance up and down Vlatko's cock. A gentle squeeze at the base of his shaft and a teasing swipe of the thumb over the head increased Vlatko's desire. He fondled Vlatko's balls with his other hand in an alternating rhythm of squeeze and tug. Vlatko knew if he allowed Rue to continue playing with him, he'd come. There was no way he'd do it. He wanted to be inside Rue's skinny ass when he spilt his seed.

He pulled Rue's hands away, causing Rue to protest. Holding Rue's arms up with one hand, Vlatko worked to strip the shirt from Rue's body with his other one. The instant Rue was naked again, Vlatko dropped the man's arms.

"Stay there," he ordered as he knelt down to feel for his pack under the cot. He jerked it from its hiding spot and opened it, searching without taking his eyes off Rue.

The thief spread his legs like a willing slut while pumping his long, curved cock. The man's amber eyes flared with orange flickers again.

"Here it is," Vlatko crowed in delight as he found the jar of lube he'd packed. He crawled up on the cot and stretched out beside Rue.

After opening the jar, he held it out. "Get yourself ready."

Something flashed in Rue's eyes and an instinct told Vlatko it wasn't anger. Even though Rue was a demanding captive, Vlatko didn't think Rue wanted to be in charge while they were fucking.

"What about protection?" Rue asked as he coated his fingers with the lube.

Vlatko shook the jar. "As well as being slick, this kind of lube acts as a sealant. No diseases in or out."

"I'll have to get some of that," Rue muttered, his eyes glazing over as he ran his hands over his balls and played with the tight pink pucker between his ass cheeks.

Vlatko pushed one of Rue's legs up and Rue grasped it behind the knee, pulling it to the side and exposing himself to Vlatko's hungry gaze.

"Do you make all your lovers do this?" Rue studied him for a moment.

Vlatko's breath caught as he breached Rue's ass with just the tip of his finger. "Only the ones I like." He ran his hand over Rue's chest and started plucking at the thief's nipples.

"Gods, that feels great." Rue arched his back, silently pleading for more.

"Two now," Vlatko instructed, his eyes glued to where Rue was finger-fucking his ass. He pinched and twisted Rue's dusky brown nipples until they were red. Vlatko enjoyed how Rue shivered every time he touched those hard nubs.

He felt the tingling at the base of his spine. His climax was rushing in on him. He slicked up his cock and moved to lie between Rue's thighs.

"It's been too long. More build-up later." He pulled Rue's fingers away.

"Fine with me." Rue placed his hands against the wall at the head of the cot. He arched his hips and grinned up at Vlatko. "I'm all yours."

Vlatko placed the blunt head of his cock at Rue's opening. He eased in as Rue pushed down. Rue's eyes were shut tight and the thief took a deep breath. Vlatko knew he was big and he hadn't given Rue a lot of time to stretch, so he took his time sliding in.

"So big." Rue bit his bottom lip as Vlatko eased another inch in.

"You're so tight." Vlatko put his hands on Rue's hips. "Take a deep breath and try to relax."

He waited until Rue started to breathe in then he pushed his full length inside.

"Don't move. Oh, gods." Rue's hands scrabbled at the wall as if he was searching for something to hold onto.

Shit! Rue'd never been this full before. Vlatko's cock was buried deep in his ass. He took another breath and braced his hands on the wall again. "Move," he ordered as he pushed down.

Vlatko laughed. "So demanding."

Rue didn't think the man was complaining. "Damn right. Now fuck me already."

"Yes, sir." Vlatko pulled out then slammed back in. The blunt head of his cock bumped Rue's gland as it went by.

"There. Again." He rocked his hips in time with Vlatko's thrusts. He planted his feet on the cot, tilting his ass at a better angle for Vlatko to fuck him harder.

The big man leant forward, kissing Rue and giving Rue's cock a hard stomach to rub against. Rue was still surprised by the kiss. He had demanded one earlier, but he'd never expected to actually get one. Men didn't kiss street thieves. It was a lesson he'd learnt when he was younger and selling his body was the only option for survival.

Vlatko didn't seem to have a problem with kissing. In fact, he did it so well Rue found he was on the edge. The combination of tongue in his mouth, hard abs rubbing on his shaft and Vlatko's thick cock pegging his gland with each thrust drove him right into the fastest climax he'd ever had.

"Fuck," he groaned as his cum shot from his cock. Lights danced in front of his eyes. His back arched and his inner muscles clamped down on Vlatko.

Vlatko grunted and shoved his shaft hard into Rue. He felt the throbbing of the thick rod as moist heat spilt from the man and filled Rue's ass.

"I'm screwed," Vlatko mumbled as the big man pulled out and collapsed at Rue's side.

Rue stretched, testing his muscles to make sure nothing had been hurt. A pleasant ache filled his body and his ass gave a spasm of lingering passion. "I think I'm the one who got screwed." He smiled as he snuggled close to Vlatko's body.

Vlatko reached and grabbed a shirt off the floor. Rue was surprised when Vlatko cleaned him off, then himself. He'd never had anyone take care of him like that.

Vlatko settled back down, pulling him tight to that massive chest, winding his arm around Rue's waist and placing his large hand on his ass.

"Rue, don't try to run. No transport is scheduled to land for another month. And I wasn't kidding about the natives killing you." Vlatko's voice rumbled under Rue's ear.

Rue gave running serious thought for a second or two. Then Vlatko squeezed his ass and Rue decided he'd stay with the person he knew. He wasn't sure what the man planned on doing about him, but Rue figured Vlatko wasn't going to kill him.

He put his hand on Vlatko's chest, feeling the man's heartbeat. A stray thought dashed through his mind before he fell asleep.

You're safe.

Chapter Two

Vlatko lay in his bed and focused on the warm body beside him. It was the thief, Rue, and the skinny man snuggled closer to him and threw one leg over his hip.

He sighed. Running a hand over Rue's back, he realised a decision would have to be made soon as to what to do with or about the man. Should he reveal what he knew about the thief or should he allow Rue to continue playing his game?

He pushed his body up to lean on his elbow, staring down at the thief. Vlatko knew who Rue was, no matter how innocent the man pretended to be. Rue was one of the best thieves in the universe. Authorities had first started paying attention to Rue when he'd been caught and branded at the age of ten. After that, Rue had never been captured again and by the time he was sixteen, he'd been commanding large sums of inter-universal credits for hired jobs.

At twenty-four, Rue still looked innocent and so young, but Vlatko knew the man could be ruthless when he needed to be. Vlatko ran a finger down over

Rue's nose. "Who paid your price for stealing the Councillor's Heart?" he wondered aloud.

"I don't know. They never tell me their names." Rue's answer was sleepy and rough.

"Ah, so you were hired to steal it for someone." Vlatko laughed.

"Shit." Rue woke, swearing and pushing away from Vlatko. "I was asleep. I don't have any idea what you're talking about."

Vlatko pressed a finger to the thief's lips. "Don't. I knew who you were the moment I saw you tied to the tree. You don't need to steal to survive anymore. You steal because someone's paying you."

Rue wanted to argue, but seemed to think better of it. "Are you going to turn me in? There's quite a bounty on my head."

Vlatko climbed out of bed. After stuffing towels and a bar of soap into a bag, he threw it into Rue's arms. Then he plucked the man off the cot.

"Where are we going?" Rue wrapped one lean arm around Vlatko's neck.

"To clean up." Vlatko shouldered open the hut's door and carried Rue to a steamy pool of water.

"Clean up? I don't see any sanitisers." Rue glanced around as Vlatko set him down next to the pool.

"You won't see one. This isn't a modern planet, Rue. In some places, indoor plumbing is still a thing of the future." Vlatko waded into the pool, holding out a hand to Rue. "Don't worry. I'll keep you safe."

The thief laughed. "Most men aren't worried about my safety. They're more concerned about getting the reward the IUM is offering."

Vlatko shrugged. "I'm not concerned with the reward." After soaking one of the cloths, he soaped it up, then proceeded to wash Rue.

Rue studied Vlatko's primitive hut and gave a disbelieving snort. "Man, you live like a homeless man. If I were you, I would have called the IUM the minute you saw my naked ass tied to that tree."

Vlatko tried to see his surroundings through Rue's eyes. So he didn't have all the comforts of modern men. His house was a two-room hut. He had very little contact with the natives, or any other people for that matter. He finished cleaning Rue. "I don't need much. Money gives you a false sense of worth."

"Spoken like a man who doesn't have any." Rue's amber eyes twinkled at him as a smile graced those plump lips.

"Maybe it's just sour grapes." He cleaned and rinsed himself. "I won't turn you in."

"Why not?"

Vlatko could tell Rue was trying to find the catch. "I don't owe the IUM anything. In fact, I'm a deserter."

"A deserter?" Rue was surprised. "If the IUM knows, why haven't they sent somebody after you?"

Anger and an odd sadness warred in Vlatko's eyes. "I think they would prefer I cease to exist, but they won't waste their time or men coming after me."

"Not to offend you or anything, but you're only one guy. I would think, if they really wanted you, they'd send a unit after you." Rue climbed out of the pool and dried off with one of the towels Vlatko had brought with them.

Vlatko followed him. Rue's gaze traced over the chiselled abs to where Vlatko's cock nestled among black curls. No doubt about it. The man was hung. Vlatko grasped the shaft, stroking it, making Rue whimper. Pre-cum glistened on the flared head of Vlatko's cock and Rue wanted to taste it.

Vlatko laid a towel on the ground at his feet. "Kneel."

Rue's brain wanted to protest the order, but his mouth and body wanted to feel Vlatko again. He dropped to his knees in front of the man. Vlatko kept stroking himself while cradling Rue's chin and lifting his gaze from the treat in front of him.

"Do you want to taste me?" Vlatko's voice was harsh and laced with passion.

Rue couldn't get his mouth to work. All it wanted to do was suck and all his tongue wanted to do was lick.

"Then enjoy breakfast."

Vlatko directed his mouth to the slick head and Rue licked the pearly drops from Vlatko's cock. Bitter and salty, it was the best thing he'd ever tasted. He sucked the tip in, teasing it with his teeth.

Vlatko warned, "Be careful."

Rue chuckled and the vibration made Vlatko growl. Rue enjoyed sucking cock. Well, he enjoyed it when he wasn't being paid to do it. Nothing killed joy more than being made to do something. Relaxing his throat, he swallowed Vlatko down until his nose was buried in the curls at the base of Vlatko's shaft.

"Shit." Vlatko combed his fingers through Rue's hair.

Rue appreciated the fact that the big man didn't force him. Rue liked commanding men who understood the difference between being forceful and forcing. Vlatko cradled the back of Rue's head while, with his other hand, he traced the hollows in Rue's cheeks as he moved up and down on the rod filling his mouth.

He looked up to see Vlatko's dark eyes staring down at him. There was a question in that gaze. He reached out, bracing his hands on Vlatko's hips, then he nodded. Vlatko gripped his head before starting to slide in and out of Rue's mouth.

Rue relaxed, shut his eyes and allowed Vlatko to fuck his mouth. He loved the velvet skin stroking his tongue. The taste of Vlatko's cum danced in his mouth. He was afraid he could get addicted to the flavour. Each time the head of Vlatko's cock hit the back of his throat, he swallowed.

"Gods, your mouth," Vlatko moaned, then started to snap his hips.

Rue slipped his hand around to cup the flexing muscles of Vlatko's ass. He stroked his fingers over the patch of skin right above Vlatko's crease.

"Rue, gonna..." Vlatko seemed to lose his interest in talking.

Rue hummed encouragement. He wanted to drink down Vlatko's cum. He wanted to suck this man dry.

The first spurt accompanied a low cry from Vlatko. Rue glanced up to see Vlatko's head thrown back, a grimace of passion marring his face. Rue closed his eyes and drank down the seed. When he'd drained every last drop, he licked the man's shaft clean and rested his head against the muscular thigh in front of him. He was so hard he knew one touch would take him over the edge.

"Come here." Vlatko reached down, grabbed Rue under the arms and lifted him until they were face to face.

Their lips met in a fierce kiss. Rue moaned as his cock rubbed against Vlatko's hard stomach. He painted a wet trail over the man's dark skin.

"Do you want my hand or my body?" Vlatko's warm breath danced on his swollen lips.

He rocked his hips, thrusting his shaft over the ridged abs. Once. Twice. His balls tightened and he knew it'd be soon.

Vlatko brushed Rue's opening and the thief exploded. His cum covered both their chests and stomachs.

"Fuck." Rue's knees went weak. He rested his head on Vlatko's shoulder, trusting Valtko to support him.

"My thoughts exactly." Vlatko chuckled and carried him back into the pool to clean off.

As he let the big man take care of him, Rue wondered what was going to happen once the shine of good sex wore off. Would Vlatko turn him in?

"Why did you run away?"

Vlatko shook his head. "You're persistent."

"That's why I'm so good at what I do." Rue gave him a wink.

"Let's go get dressed." Vlatko headed back to his hut after gathering up the towels and soap.

"Then you'll tell me why you're here and not in some IUM prison." The thief walked beside him with a loose stride.

"Maybe." Vlatko didn't want to go into the whole reason why he'd chosen to desert. He didn't really want to relive the life-changing moment when he'd realised he couldn't be a solider anymore.

"Maybe? Hey, I told you the truth about stealing the Councillor's Heart. Where's the respect? Give and take here. I give you something. You give me something in return." Rue glanced at him. "What's for breakfast?"

"You already had your breakfast." Vlatko leered at the man. Opening the hut's door, he gestured for Rue to go in ahead of him. He reached out and pinched the guy's ass as he went by.

"You know, I shouldn't let you get away with that. You shouldn't be able to touch me without giving me something in return." Rue frowned.

Vlatko laughed. "So now you want to negotiate. We're bartering sex for my secrets." He stopped to think about it for a second. "Not sure it'd be worth it, from my point of view."

"Not worth it? I fucking blew your mind out there." Rue's outrage was cute.

He rubbed a thumb over the frown between Rue's eyes. "Yes, you did, little thief, but I have a problem sharing my secrets with a man I've just met."

"But no problem with sharing your body?" Rue threw himself down on the cot, crossed his arms and glared at Vlatko.

Vlatko had been in the middle of pulling out plates and pots to make breakfast. He turned to stare at Rue. "Did I miss something? When did you turn into a woman?"

"What the hell?" Rue sounded offended.

"We had sex, but we didn't declare our undying love for each other. Why this need to know my deepest, darkest secrets? You don't see me pushing you to tell me your life story." Vlatko cracked a couple of eggs into the frying pan.

Rue sighed. "You're right. I tend to get this way after I've gotten close to getting caught and maybe dying." The thief stood behind him and wrapped those skinny arms around his waist. "You don't have to tell me anything, Vlatko. I do know how to just fuck."

Vlatko scrambled the eggs then slid them on some plates while he thought about his past. He'd never wanted to tell anyone why he'd chosen the path he'd taken.

"Go sit down." He waved towards his small table with two chairs. "Would you like water or something stronger to drink? I don't have visitors very often, so I don't have much."

Rue tugged on one of Vlatko's shirts before sitting. "Water's fine."

Vlatko set a plate and a glass in front of Rue then joined the thief. "Do you pay attention to the news?" He pushed the eggs on his plate around with his fork.

Rue moaned around the first forkful. "Sure I do. I need to keep up with possible jobs and to see if someone might be talking about me." Rue shovelled another mouthful. "Where the hell did you get real eggs?"

Vlatko chuckled. "I told you this was a primitive planet. They grow most of their food."

"No wonder you stay here." Rue's glance shot over to Vlatko's food.

"Here, I'm not hungry." Vlatko shoved his plate across the table. Leaning back, he played with his glass while watching Rue eat. "About four years ago, there was a big dust-up in the news about a high-level IUM officer being shot in cold blood by one of his subordinates."

Rue stopped chewing for a second, staring at him. "I remember. It was around the same time I boosted the Rouge diamond from the museum on Ecofo."

"So that was you. I always wondered." He added 'ballsy' to his mental list of traits Rue had.

"Yep. Got a pretty penny for the bauble when I sold it. So were you the subordinate who pulled the trigger?" There didn't seem to be any worry on Rue's face or in his voice.

"No. I'm the assassin the IUM sent after the subordinate to kill him. The official word was dead or alive, but unofficially I had to kill him." Vlatko's words were flat and cold.

Rue felt his mouth drop open. Shit. Vlatko was an assassin. This changed everything. "So did you find the fugitive and kill him?" He wasn't sure about what he'd been expecting to hear, but it certainly wasn't what Vlatko had said.

"Yes." Vlatko gathered the empty plates and set them in the sink.

"If you did what they asked you to do, why are you a deserter?" Rue frowned.

Vlatko moved to stand in the doorway, staring out into the forest. "I learnt too much. I saw too much." The big man looked down at his hand. "When your hands are stained red by all the blood spilt, you began to question everything. Other issues arose to make me decide getting away from them was best for me."

"And the IUM doesn't like questions." Rue climbed to his feet, then joined Vlatko at the door.

Vlatko shook his head. "It wasn't the IUM I was questioning. I knew they were wrong. I never volunteered to be their trained killer. I was born into it."

Fuck. Rue's head was starting to hurt. "If you didn't doubt them, what the hell did you doubt?"

Vlatko sighed. "It doesn't make sense, I know, but I doubted everything. Why do we fight so hard to live?"

Rue followed Vlatko as the man wandered back towards the clearing where Rue had been tied the day before. "We fight because the only other option is lying down and dying." Rue reached out to take Vlatko's hand.

Vlatko glanced over at him, but didn't pull his hand away. "Why? Why are we living? Are we supposed to learn something?"

Rue started laughing. "The IUM must have freaked out when their trained assassin turned into a philosopher."

Vlatko smiled. "IUM freaked because I told them I had files and information, not only on the most recent mission, but on all the people they sent me to kill."

They walked into the clearing and stopped in front of the firebird's tree. The creature screeched at them as sparks rained down from her feathers. The bird's plumage was brilliant red and orange, as if the creature were on fire. Another ear-piercing scream ricocheted through the clearing.

"Hush, you old fraud," Vlatko called out to her.

Rue found himself jerked up against Vlatko's body. He stared up into Vlatko's black eyes. "You're covering your ass by blackmailing them into letting you go." He rubbed his thumb over Vlatko's bottom lip.

"Yeah and I never thought they'd send such a sexy thief to steal them from me."

Rue felt his heart stop.

Vlatko didn't know if the shocked expression on Rue's face was because he'd been found out or because Vlatko had figured it out so soon.

"I don't know what you're talking about. I'm not here to steal anything from you." Rue struggled in his arms.

"Excuse me if I don't believe that." He gestured to where a bag sat just at the edge of the clearing. "I left the hut while you were sleeping and did a little exploring. Found your bag in the bushes there.

Clothes, credits and a pretty little red stone. The Councillor's Heart is beautiful. If you were tied up here by someone who wasn't happy with you, he wouldn't have left you anything. But all your stuff is right there."

He pushed Rue towards the bag. The thief stumbled across the hard ground and Vlatko fought the urge to help him. Shaking his head, he moved towards the tree where the firebird still perched. The closer he got, the more agitated the bird became, until sparks rained down like a little meteor shower. The embers stung his skin, but he didn't move away.

"I figured they would send someone. The information I have could topple a few governments if the universe found out the truth. It's dangerous for me to still be alive." He turned to see Rue pulling on some pants and a dark green, chest-hugging shirt. He continued in a thoughtful tone. "If I had friends, I'd be led to believe that the IUM talked to them about the best way to get me to lower my guard."

Rue started to say something, but Vlatko held up his hand. "Don't get me wrong. I never wanted friends. Life is far easier without worrying about other people. Friends can be used against you. But so can nature."

Vlatko lifted his hand higher, bringing it within reach of the shrieking bird. She struck out with her beak. He kept his eyes on Rue, ignoring the danger above him. One foot gripped his wrist and he grimaced at the smell of burning flesh.

"Wait. Don't let that thing touch you. You'll get fried." Rue stood up, holding out his hand as if wanting to stop Vlatko.

"There are benefits to being a trained killer, Rue. One is liquid body armour they inject under your skin. It makes you impervious to fire, guns and anything short of a nuclear explosion." The second claw closed around his wrist and he brought the bird down. "The only discomfort I have is from the smell. The top layer of my flesh will grow back."

Rue was glancing wildly around the clearing. Vlatko watched the lean muscles tense and he knew Rue was planning on running. He hid a smile. The IUM hadn't briefed the thief very well if the guy thought he could survive on the planet long enough for someone to rescue him.

"Don't run, Rue. I was telling the truth. There are only the primitive people of the planet and they give me a wide berth." He worked the transmitter out of his pocket with his free hand. "And I took the liberty of stealing your transmitter. The IUM won't send anyone in to save you. You should have done more research before you accepted this job, Rue."

Chapter Three

Rue couldn't believe it. He'd never been found out before. He smiled to himself. Of course, he'd never gone up against a stone-cold killer like Vlatko. Glancing around the clearing, he wondered if Vlatko was telling the truth. His eyes settled on the dark man and the flaming bird he held.

"That has to hurt, man." It wasn't what he wanted to say but his tongue-brain connection had been interrupted by shock.

Those dark eyes watched him, ignoring the striking beak of the bird. "Not really. With all the bonuses the body armour gives me, the drawback is a loss of nerve endings. I don't usually feel pain, or pleasure for the matter."

"Don't feel pain or pleasure? That's seriously fucked up." Rue shook his head. "But you seemed to be fine earlier."

"Makes sense, doesn't it? If you want a ruthless assassin, you've got to make him pain-free. Deaden his nerve endings. Bingo. Got a killer." Vlatko lifted his arm, forcing the firebird to step off onto a branch.

"As to the pleasure, who knows why it worked for you and me. It hasn't always worked for me before."

Rue tensed. Here was where Vlatko grabbed him and killed him. He hoped Sysu enjoyed the money he'd left him. He figured his associate wouldn't waste any time emptying out the bank accounts when Rue didn't return. Vlatko moved back in the direction of the hut.

"Wait. Aren't you going to kill me?" Rue snapped his mouth shut. *Damn. No need to give the man suggestions.*

Vlatko grinned over a broad shoulder at him. "Rue, I knew before you woke up this morning why you were really here. I could have gotten rid of you without any trouble then. I prefer not to kill anymore."

Rue was dumbfounded. He hadn't thought about that. Vlatko could have easily broken his neck with those big hands. "Why?"

The man shrugged. "Boredom, I think. You've been the most fun I've had since I landed on this planet. Listen, I don't plan on killing you, so relax. I'll give you four weeks to try and find the information. Afterwards, if you haven't found them, I'll let you contact whomever you want."

"Even if it's the IUM?"

"Um... The IUM might be sending a unit in to capture you. Stealing the Councillor's Heart is a big deal." Vlatko held the ruby up.

"It's not the Councillor's Heart. The agent I met who gave me the details for this job said the jewel I'd be stealing was a plant. It's all part of the cover story." A sick feeling rolled over him when Vlatko shook his head.

"Never trust the IUM. The men who run it will screw you over as soon as they can. They have a combination of reasons why they wanted the Heart stolen. One, Mitcov is an independent amber planet. Without the Heart, they'll get into trouble and the IUM can move in to save them. And two, it gives you a reason to end up on my planet. Maybe the universally famous Rue can find the files when no one else can. I'm pretty sure the IUM arranged for that cargo ship to be the only one available for you to steal away on. You knew you were going to be taken somewhere to try and steal some files. You just didn't know how it was going to happen, and who you were supposed to take from." Vlatko strolled over to him to cup his face.

He swallowed. It wasn't a good idea, but hell, he'd never been good. Rising up on his toes, he pressed his lips against Vlatko's.

Vlatko nibbled on Rue's mouth. Maybe it was crazy not to kill the thief right then, but he didn't care. His files were hidden in the one place Rue would never find them. He placed kisses along Rue's chin, heading to the sensitive spot behind the slender man's ear. Scraping his teeth over skin, he chuckled when Rue shivered and pressed closer to him. He slid his hands down to cup Rue's firm ass. Vlatko picked Rue up and carried him to the nearest tree.

Vlatko set the man down and pushed him until Rue was leaning back against the trunk. He grasped those bony wrists, lifting them above Rue's blond head. "Keep them up. No touching."

Rue whimpered, small perfect white teeth biting that swollen bottom lip. "All right."

He placed a gentle kiss on Rue's nose. "I won't hurt you. Trust me." Those strange amber eyes rolled and Vlatko realised how stupid the request sounded. "I haven't hurt you yet. I've only brought you pleasure and I plan on doing that again."

He palmed Rue's cock through the man's pants, then squeezed. With his eyes closed, Rue let his head fall back and a groan issued from his bared throat.

Vlatko teased Rue, fondling and rubbing the man's shaft. He leant down, taking a nip at the point where the neck and collarbone met.

"Again. More. Harder." He'd reduced Rue to single word sentences. His bony hips rolled into each touch. "Please."

"Please what?" Vlatko breathed in Rue's ear, licking the outside edge.

"Touch me." Begging sounded good from the thief.

"I am touching you." He moved his other hand back to mould and knead Rue's ass.

"Skin. Skin on skin. Yours on mine."

"Rather pushy, aren't you?" But Vlatko was willing to do as Rue demanded.

He managed to unbutton Rue's pants with one hand, keeping the other playing with Rue's backside. He didn't want the man to start thinking and decide this wasn't a good idea. Though the way Rue was moaning and shivering, Vlatko didn't think the man could form a rational thought at the moment.

Their groans joined together as Vlatko's hand engulfed the hot, velvety-hard shaft that undoing Rue's pants revealed. He gripped it firmly and pumped down, then up. Rue's body moved with his strokes. Vlatko sucked up a spot on Rue's neck, worrying it with teeth and tongue.

"Damn." Rue's hands scrabbled against the tree bark.

Vlatko pushed his other hand down the back of Rue's pants to play with the top of the man's crease.

"Oh, gods," Rue cried out.

Vlatko reached down and rolled Rue's balls in his hand. They were tight and he knew he could make the man come with just his hands, but he had the sudden urge to taste the thief. Sucking cock wasn't something he liked to do—maybe it was just too intimate a thing. Yet there was a need in him to take Rue's shaft in his mouth and drink from him.

He knelt before Rue, wrapping his hand around the base of Rue's long slender cock and licking the flared head. Rue almost levitated. His wild cry echoed through the clearing, causing Vlatko to smile. At least the thief liked that, so Vlatko set to work. He traced the large, throbbing vein along the underside of Rue's shaft with his tongue. He took the head into his mouth and swirled his tongue over it, tasting the bitter saltiness of Rue's pre-cum. Pulling off, he saw Rue staring down at him, need and pleasure bursting in the man's eyes.

"Ready?" He didn't wait for Rue to answer. He swallowed the man down while at the same time, he pressed his finger into Rue's ass.

Rue came undone, thrusting and crying out. The man started fucking Vlatko's face while Vlatko finger-fucked him.

"Gonna…" Rue warned.

Vlatko hummed around the shaft in his mouth, wanting to taste Rue. The vibration from his hum must have been too much as Rue came with a shout, his cum flooding Vlatko's mouth. Vlatko swallowed as much as he could, but a little found freedom at the corner of his lips. He licked and sucked until Rue stood quietly before him. With one last swipe to make sure the man's shaft was clean, he climbed to his feet.

Rue's eyes were stunned. The slender man reached up and wiped the drop of his cum off Vlatko's chin. Vlatko watched Rue suck it from his finger. Rue wrapped his arms around his neck and pulled him into a kiss that said 'thank you' and 'more, please'. There was another emotion in the kiss, but he didn't recognise it and didn't care. He encircled the thief's waist and let Rue rest on him.

"What about you?" Rue patted Vlatko's cock.

"I'm fine." It was the truth. He didn't ache or need at the moment. At least not for sex.

"Okay." Rue's eyes closed and his head came to rest on Vlatko's shoulder.

Vlatko lowered them to the ground under the oak tree, manoeuvring so Rue could use him for a mattress. He didn't want Rue to be stiff when he woke up from his nap. Running his hand through Rue's blond curls, he laughed at himself. Maybe it wasn't boredom making him keep the thief alive. Maybe something else was at work here. He glanced up at the firebird peering down from her perch. He swore the bird winked at him.

* * * *

The first thing Rue saw when he opened his eyes was the firebird glaring down at him from her perch. A voice in the back of his head yelled for him to run. To get away while he still could. He couldn't remember why, and since Vlatko seemed to have sucked his brain out through his cock, he didn't have the intelligence to figure out where to run.

"You're awake and trying to remember why every instinct you have is screaming for you to run." Vlatko sat down next to him and ran a hand over his hair.

"How did you know?" Rue rested his head on Vlatko's thigh, staring up at the man.

"You had a dazed 'What the hell do I do now?' look." Vlatko chuckled.

"If you're right, why did the IUM choose me to steal the files from you?" He opened his mouth and nibbled on the piece of apple Vlatko had sliced for him.

"Not sure how they did it, but the guys in the Secrets branch of the military must have figured out my weakness." Vlatko handled the sharp steel blade deftly.

Rue knew he should be worried the knife would slip and he'd find himself dead. Yet he believed Vlatko wasn't going to kill him. Of course, that could be wishful thinking. "Your weakness?"

"Slender, pretty men with bad attitudes." Vlatko winked at him.

"Strange. Large dark men were never my thing." Rue rubbed his cheek against the front of Vlatko's pants.

"There's always a first time, baby. You came here for the challenge. They used your ego against you. You had to prove how good you are by stealing something from one of the IUM's trained killers." Vlatko shook his head. "I always knew egos could get people into trouble."

"You don't have an ego?" Rue took another piece of apple.

"No. I know I'm good, but I don't have to prove it to everyone who questions me."

Rue threw a quick glance over the muscular body close to him. "Who would question you? Even I would think twice about it."

"There's been one or two."

"Why didn't you kill me?" Rue hated coming back to that question, but his mind wouldn't let go of it.

"I don't kill anymore." Vlatko tucked the knife away in the fabric of his clothes.

"Why? I can't believe you woke up one morning and said 'I'm done'. Did you kill someone you didn't think should die?"

Vlatko's smile sent a lustful heat racing to Rue's groin and a cold shiver down his spine.

"None of the people I killed deserved to die, but I killed them anyway, Rue. I didn't suddenly grow a conscience." Vlatko stroked Rue's throat. "You'll probably think I'm a monster, but I liked killing. I liked the power and the thrill of the hunt."

"Then why walk away and make yourself a marked man?" Rue understood the thrill and the seduction of power, but he didn't understand walking away from what made the man happy, even if it was killing others.

"I got tired of being used. The men who run the IUM don't want to get their own hands dirty, so they turn other men into hunters and executioners. I believe they need to take responsibility for their own actions. They need to be the ones pulling the trigger or holding the knife." Vlatko stared off over the clearing. "The thing they didn't imagine was their created killer would start thinking for himself. Their overwhelming problem is they think they're far more intelligent than every other person in the universe."

"It must have shocked them when you told them no, then let them know you had proof of what they did." Rue's muscles were relaxing under Vlatko's touch. He squashed the stray thought that with one squeeze of those fingers his throat could be crushed.

"Their faces turned red and then white. I walked out of the room with them staring daggers at my back." Vlatko shrugged. "It didn't bother me. They've feared me since the day they made me."

"If I were smart, I'd fear you too." Rue grinned.

"You are smart and you are afraid of me, but your instincts are starting to kick in and tell you I won't hurt you. I really have nothing to gain by killing you."

Vlatko reached down and pulled him up, so Rue knelt, facing the man. Vlatko stroked his rough thumb over the tender spot behind Rue's ear, making him moan.

"I get the feeling I'd lose more than I ever thought possible if I killed you."

Vlatko's words and warm breath settling over his lips caused another shiver to race down Rue's spine, but this one wasn't caused by fear.

Vlatko tasted the fresh tang of the apple from Rue's lips. He licked along the plump bottom lip then sank his tongue in Rue's mouth. Keeping the kiss gentle and not letting it get out of hand was tough, but Vlatko wanted to do more than just fuck Rue. However, they would be doing more of that. For the first time in his life, Vlatko wanted to get to know someone just for the sake of knowing them. He had no other reason for it.

Rue encircled his neck and pushed his lean body tighter to him. Vlatko reached down, cupping his firm ass, then lifting to create a better angle for the kiss. When their breath ran out, they pulled apart and stood staring at each other.

"We should head back and grab some lunch. I think we both worked up an appetite." He grinned at Rue.

"You're right." Rue's stomach growled and they laughed. "So what do you do on this planet?"

Vlatko wasn't ready to tell Rue what he was really doing on this unnamed planet. "I made arrangements with the king. I provide protection for his hunting parties and he leaves me alone."

"You have to be bored out of your fucking mind." Rue glanced around as they made their way back to the hut.

"Maybe I like the solitude. It might be a great place for me to contemplate my guilt."

Vlatko bit back a smile when Rue stared at him in astonishment then doubled over in laughter.

"I can almost believe the solitude part, since you don't strike me as an extrovert, but don't try to convince me the guilty conscience bullshit is true." Rue chuckled.

"Okay, so I don't wallow in the 'I'm a horrible person' pit." Vlatko opened the hut door, studying Rue as he ushered him in.

He'd given Rue a month to find the files, and it would only be a matter of time before Rue found the trapdoor in the process of his search. So he might as well let Rue in on that part of the secret.

"When I'm not doing escort duty, I'm usually down here."

Pushing the bed out of the way, Vlatko revealed a trapdoor. He unsealed it and hauled the door up, gesturing for Rue to climb down. He followed.

"Holy shit."

They stood in a large chamber equipped with everything a modern house would have on another planet. A kitchen, bathroom and bedroom branched off the main room. Vlatko's computers lined the far wall.

"Would you like something to eat?" Vlatko reached for the refrigerator door.

"Shouldn't you bandage that?" Rue gestured to the burn marks on Vlatko's wrist.

"I'm immune to every known infection and disease. My healing rate is faster than a normal human's." He pulled out the fixings for sandwiches.

"Pretty handy." Rue settled on a chair at the table.

"The IUM spent a lot of credits and time on making me into the perfect killer." He poured glasses of water.

"They must have thrown fits when their million credit machine walked out on them." Rue took a sip.

"They did, but since the IUM has several more just like me, they aren't too worried about it. It is the information I have that they fear." Vlatko knew the thief was trying to scope the place without letting Vlatko know about it. He could see those amber eyes dart from one corner to the other. Rue wouldn't be able to find anything. "You can throw all the credits in the universe into creating a person like me, but all those same credits couldn't get me to stay." He set the plate on the table between them.

"True, but what's to stop them from making another just like you?" Rue grabbed a sandwich and took a bite.

"They can't make more of us because it seems all their research has disappeared." He winked at Rue.

A ringing sound came from one of the computers then a voice blared into the room.

"Hey, Iceman, this is Stargazer. You ready for me to land?"

Rue's eyebrows rose. "So, Iceman, who's Stargazer?"

"A colleague. He supplies me with items I can't get here on the planet." Vlatko smiled at him and headed towards one of the computers. "Stargazer. Ready as always. Be advised I have a visitor."

"Is he pretty?" A harsh chuckle came over the speaker.

Goose bumps rose on Rue's skin. He didn't know if they were from unease or interest in the rough masculine voice talking to Vlatko.

"As pretty as the firebird." Vlatko's dark eyes ran over Rue, making the thief feel as if the man had stripped him naked.

"Can't wait to see for myself. That bird of yours burns brightly. Meet me at the landing strip." The intercom went silent.

Vlatko headed to a door opposite the computer wall. He opened it and took a step inside, pausing to look back over his shoulder at Rue. "Aren't you coming?"

Rue was surprised. He'd figured Vlatko wouldn't want him to know where the landing strip was. "You want me to go with you?"

A puzzled frown marred Vlatko's forehead. "Why wouldn't I?"

"When I find the files, I'll be able to contact the IUM to pick me up and having a landing strip would make it easier. They'll be able to get at you whenever they want." He joined Vlatko in the narrow hallway.

"True, but since you're not going to find my files, I'm not worried about what other knowledge you gain. You might want to reconsider contacting the IUM when you're ready to leave. They did set you up, after all."

Vlatko led the way down the dark corridor. The lights were motion operated, turning on when they approached and going dark after they passed.

"I thought you said there wouldn't be a transport for another month," Rue accused.

"I lied. There won't be another commercial transport for a month. Stargazer's ship isn't commercial and he wouldn't take you. No matter how pretty you are." Vlatko stopped at the base of a steel ladder. "I'll go first." He started to climb.

"Why wouldn't he take me?" Rue followed.

"He's trying to stay under the IUM's radar." Vlatko's voice drifted down to him.

"Yet he's helping you." Rue blinked in the burst of light created when Vlatko opened a hatch at the top of the ladder. "It doesn't seem very 'under the radar' to me."

"It is considering Stargazer is the oath-brother to the last man I killed."

Vlatko reached down and pulled a stunned Rue up through the hatch. Rue found himself standing in the corner of an enormous cave whose mouth was wide enough for a small ship to fit through. A rather nondescript ship rested on the landing pad already.

A pale man stalked towards them. An inch or two shorter than Rue, the confident way the stranger walked and met Rue's gaze made him seem larger.

"Why?" was all he could think of to say.

Chapter Four

"Why would I have anything to do with the man who killed my oath-brother and lover?" The pale man stopped in front of the thief.

Vlatko saw how Stargazer studied Rue. Oh yeah, there was interest there. Since he didn't know how Rue would react to a move from the other man, Vlatko wasn't going to give his friend permission to touch the thief. A frown forced its way over Vlatko's face. He'd never been possessive of his lovers. In his life, he'd joined in more than his share of threesomes, but something bothered him at the thought of Stargazer touching Rue.

"Yeah. I mean Vlatko fucking killed the man you loved. Wouldn't your partner have been pissed off as hell at your helping his killer out?" Rue moved ever so slightly towards Vlatko.

It wasn't like he'd been looking for a sign, but the movement made Vlatko feel better. He caught the pale man's gaze and shook his head, placing his hand on the small of Rue's back.

Stargazer nodded, moving back to where his men were off-loading some boxes. "Mal was a hothead. I told him we'd handle the problem without killing anyone, but he ran out and shot the officer. Iceman was just doing his job. Can't get mad at a man doing what he's ordered to do. I want revenge on the men who sent Vlatko to kill Mal."

"So the best revenge is working with their hired killer?" Rue leaned against Vlatko, letting the big man support his weight.

"It's not like I can kill Iceman. Not talented enough for it." Stargazer winked. "Besides it'd be a waste of a perfectly good man to kill him."

"Are you here for a long visit or is this a short stop?" Vlatko eased his fingers under Rue's shirt and stroked a thumb over the soft spot right above the thief's ass.

Rue shivered, pressing tighter to him. Vlatko wanted to bend down and lick the skin behind Rue's ear. Would it taste as good as it did when he was fucking the man?

"Just a short stop. Dropping off a few supplies." Stargazer's eyes were hot when they met Vlatko's. "Besides, I don't want to interrupt your fun."

Vlatko dipped his fingers below Rue's waistband to tease the top of Rue's crease. The thief jumped and bit his bottom lip.

"If you two need to talk, I'll go back to Vlatko's." Rue's voice was heavy with desire.

Both Vlatko and Stargazer shook their heads.

"No need, pretty. I'll chat with our big friend here later. My guys are done." Stargazer clapped his hand to Vlatko's shoulder. "I hope you know what you're doing, friend."

"Don't worry. It'll be okay." Vlatko touched his forehead softly to the shorter man's. "Safe journey and I'll talk to you soon."

Rue and Vlatko moved back towards the hatch. They stood, watching the small transport lift off and fly out of the cave. As soon as Stargazer's ship was out of sight, Vlatko pushed Rue up against the stone wall and took his lips in a fierce kiss. Rue gasped and Vlatko took advantage, plunging his tongue into the moist cavern of the thief's mouth. He cupped the firm, leather-covered ass and lifted the man up so their groins fit together.

He timed their movements to coincide with the thrusts of his tongue into Rue's mouth. It would have been better if they were naked, but he didn't want to take the time for that. He wanted to make Rue come then he was going to fuck the man's pretty little ass.

Rue gripped his shoulders before throwing his head back and groaning. "Vlatko, I'm going to…"

"I know. That's it." He growled and bit the tendon in Rue's neck.

Rue jerked and cried out. Vlatko let the man drop. With fumbling hands, he managed to get Rue's pants open and pushed down, baring the man's ass. After whirling the thief around, he pressed Rue's chest against the wall.

"Please," Rue begged, tilting his hips and offering his body to Vlatko.

Vlatko dug a small bottle of slick out of his pocket before ripping open his own pants to coat his cock. He slid one lubed finger into Rue's ass, burning with lust when the man hissed at the intrusion. Without finesse, he stretched and relaxed Rue's hole, making him ready to take Vlatko's cock.

"Now," Rue demanded, pushing back on Vlatko's fingers.

Vlatko pulled out and placed his cock at the opening. No hesitation. He pushed in as deep as he could go. Rue almost climbed the wall, crying out. Vlatko grabbed the thin hips and started impaling the man on his shaft. Rue's inner muscles milked his cock and he could feel his balls draw up. It wouldn't take long for his orgasm to hit him. He'd been close to the edge when he'd made Rue come. Yet he'd held off because he'd wanted to be buried in the man before he spilt his seed.

"Vlatko, please." Rue's voice was harsh.

Vlatko peeled one hand off Rue's hip and reached around to grasp the man's cock. It was hard and all it took was two pumps to make Rue shoot again.

"Shit," Vlatko grunted as Rue's inner channel contracted tightly around his shaft. As Rue's warm cum coated his hand, Vlatko emptied his load into the man's ass, swearing with each thrust. He collapsed, pinning the smaller man against the wall while he tried to catch his breath.

Rue whimpered when Vlatko pulled out of his ass. Vlatko grabbed a rag resting on a box. After cleaning off, he fastened his pants before wiping Rue off. He turned the thief around, then pulled his leather pants up to button them. Vlatko placed a soft kiss on Rue's swollen lips.

The fire in those amber eyes faded while he watched and he found himself remembering Stargazer's comment. He didn't know what the fuck he was doing in the overall grand scheme of things. He was taking a chance Rue wouldn't figure out where the files were being kept.

Rue gave him a shy smile and Vlatko realised he knew what he was doing at the moment. He'd be doing Rue again until the man's ass was sore and it was uncomfortable for him to sit down for the next day.

Rue didn't think he would be able to make it down the ladder into the tunnel. His legs were as limp as noodles. He studied the opening in the floor.

"I'll go first. That way if you slip, I'll be there to catch you." Vlatko backed down the rungs while smiling up at him.

He stared down into the dark eyes of the killer and wondered why he trusted Vlatko. He'd only known this man for two days, yet he knew Vlatko would catch him. From the moment he'd opened his eyes to see Vlatko standing in front of him, his trust had grown. It didn't matter what the man had done before they'd met. He didn't even care if Vlatko was still being used as a killer by the IUM. The more time he spent with Vlatko, the more he hoped he didn't find the files. Some part of him wanted to stay and figure out what made Vlatko tick.

"Are you coming?" Vlatko's voice drifted up from the bottom of the ladder.

"Yes." He moved to join him. After reaching the bottom, he leaned against the wall and sighed.

"Wore you out, huh?" Vlatko grinned at him. "Don't worry. I've got you." The man bent down and swept Rue up in his arms.

Rue embraced Vlatko, resting his head on the man's broad shoulders. He counted the doors leading off the tunnel as they made their way back to the underground chambers. There were five of them and he knew he'd be investigating all of them before the month was up.

"So what's in those rooms?" he asked, but didn't expect to get an answer.

"Supplies in four of them. The fifth? I guess you'll have to pick the lock to find out." Vlatko chuckled. "Of course, the lock requires a retinal scan and a voice imprint. You're the best thief in the universe, so I'm sure you've had to deal with that type of security before. I can't wait to see how you handle that."

"I'll find a way in. I haven't found a door yet I couldn't break." He winked up at Vlatko. "They don't call me the best for nothing."

Vlatko's deep laugh followed them as they went through the main living space into the bedroom. Rue was ashamed to admit he squeaked as Vlatko tossed him onto the bed. He scrambled around, trying not to get tangled in the sheets

"I'm going to take a shower. Maybe you'd like to rest for a little bit. It's been an exhausting morning." Vlatko walked away from him, stripping his clothes off with each step.

"With real water?" Rue sprang off the bed, then rushed after the man's tight ass. All the showers he'd ever taken were with sanitizers, which were just sprays of disinfectants and chemicals. None had ever been in real water. Though Rue didn't know why he was surprised by Vlatko using water, since they'd soaked in the pools earlier.

"Of course real water. I might have sacrificed the luxuries of living on a more modern planet, but I gained the wonders of a primitive world. One of which is fresh, clean water." Vlatko led the way into the adjoining bathroom where he bent over to turn the water on.

Rue couldn't stop his hands from groping the firm muscles presented to him as he went into the room. Vlatko arched and pushed back into Rue's hands. Rue flexed his fingers, massaging and teasing. The big man straightened, turning to grasp Rue's chin in his hand and crush a kiss to his mouth.

Rue gasped, and slid his hands from Vlatko's ass to fist the hard cock rising proudly from the strong thighs and black curls at his groin. He nibbled along Vlatko's jaw while stroking the flesh in his grip.

Steam rose from the hot water and sweat beaded upon their skin. He tasted the salt at the base of Vlatko's neck. Rue licked a line down the middle of the man's chest and over Vlatko's ripped abs. Dropping to his knees, he followed the crease by the hip until the leaking tip of Vlatko's cock hit Rue's chin. He sucked Vlatko's head into his mouth and hummed at the liquid drops of pre-cum coating his tongue.

"I love your mouth," Vlatko moaned and thrust his cock deeper into Rue's mouth.

Rue wanted to say how much he loved Vlatko's dick, but he was more interested in sucking every last drop he could out of the man. He closed his eyes, relaxed his muscles and swallowed until Vlatko's cock hit the back of his throat.

A shout rang through the room and Vlatko grabbed his head, holding him still as he thrust in and out of Rue's mouth. He braced his hands on Vlatko's hips, allowing Vlatko to fuck his face.

"I'm gonna come, babe." Vlatko's voice was harsh.

The first salty bitter burst of cum flooded his mouth.

Vlatko locked his knees to keep from crumbling to the floor as the last drops of his cum filled Rue's mouth. His chin dropped forward and rested on his chest. He stared down at the slender man smiling back at him. He stroked his fingers through the blond hair curling in the steam.

"Stand up and I'll take care of you in the shower." He stepped back to allow Rue room to stand up.

"No need. I came when you did." Rue gave him a grin.

Vlatko pressed a gentle kiss to Rue's mouth while manoeuvring Rue under the hot water. He scrubbed his own body quickly, letting Rue touch him wherever he wanted to with his clever hands. After rinsing off the soap, Vlatko reached for Rue. He took his time, learning every inch of the soft skin and hard muscles making up the intriguing, lean body. He figured out which spots made Rue sigh and which made him shiver. By the time the water ran cold, Rue was bracing himself against Vlatko and moaning.

"The water's getting cold and I think you're ready for a nap." Vlatko shut off the water before lifting Rue.

Rue mumbled something, but Vlatko couldn't make it out. He laughed, drying Rue with soft strokes and light touches. He tossed the towel on the counter then picked the thief up in his arms. Vlatko tucked Rue under the covers and kissed him on the forehead.

"Rest. I'll get you up before dinner."

Rue cradled Vlatko's cheek for a moment and gave him an endearing smile. "Thank you."

"You're welcome."

Vlatko shut the bedroom door and wandered over to the bank of computers on the opposite wall. Typing in a code, he called up the security camera he'd installed in the bedroom. He would be able to keep an eye on the thief without staying with him. Vlatko didn't need more than an hour or two of sleep a day. One more marvellous improvement in the genetic code of a killer.

He pulled a chair over before sitting. One of the other computer screens blinked on. While Rue slept, he'd have time to work on his research. Somewhere in the crowd of numbers and codes, he knew he'd find the answer to his problem.

Thirty minutes into his work, he stopped to stare at the picture of Rue. He couldn't concentrate. Even when the man was sleeping, there was something about the thief that drew him in. Vlatko tugged the Councillor's Heart from his pocket and rubbed it with his fingers.

The IUM had known what they were doing when they hired Rue to steal the jewel. Mitcov was one of the few independent planets left on the outskirts of the universe. The red stone Vlatko held was the key to their survival. How or why, he didn't know, but without it Mitcov would have to bend to the demands of the IUM. He wasn't sure what he should do about it. If he had any sort of conscience, he'd contact Stargazer and have the man retrieve it. Stargazer would return the stone to the rightful owners—for a price, of course.

Vlatko shook his head. It wasn't his call to make. Rue would have to decide what to do with the stone. The thief had been hired to steal it, so it was his job. Vlatko wouldn't like it if Rue told him how to kill, and he didn't think Rue would enjoy Vlatko sticking his nose in where it didn't belong.

He stood and headed towards the tunnel. He'd put the stone in the secure room. Rue would figure out how to break into it before he left, but Vlatko wasn't worried. In truth, he didn't keep anything of importance in the room except for a little of his money and some weapons. The room was a distraction, along with the computers. All the critical information, weapons and majority of his wealth were hidden where no one — not even the best thief in the universe — could find them.

After putting the stone away, he went back to work. He needed to find the answer because time was running out and Vlatko realised he'd just found a more compelling reason to succeed than getting revenge on the IUM. He touched a fingertip to the screen showing Rue sleeping in his bed.

Chapter Five

Two weeks left

Rue stood in the middle of the fourth storage room. The security had been an example of simplicity. He'd been picking locks of that calibre since he was ten. The instant he'd seen the four doors, he'd known he wasn't going to find the files in the rooms. Vlatko was too smart a man to trust the underground chamber wouldn't be discovered, so the killer wouldn't leave anything he really thought was valuable there.

With a frustrated sigh, he put all the supply boxes back where he'd found them. Rue shut the door, locking it before he made his way down the hall to the main living room. The fifth locked door drew his attention. He hadn't found a way to crack it yet, but he still had two more weeks to figure it out.

"Vlatko must trust you an awful lot."

The voice from down the hall made Rue jump. He turned to see Stargazer smiling at him.

"I think he trusts his safeguards more than me. What are you doing back already?"

"I forgot to drop off some supplies last time. Thought I'd run them back, since I was in the area." Stargazer moved closer to him.

Rue saw the interest flare in the pale man's eyes and an idea rushed through his head. "Vlatko is out with a hunting party. Would you like a drink?"

He turned and sauntered to the main living room. He made sure that with each step, his hips swayed, drawing Stargazer's eyes. He would use the lust Vlatko's partner felt for him to get information.

"Made yourself at home, I see." Stargazer moved up behind Rue and brushed a hand over his ass.

Rue pushed back, just enough to encourage the man. He reached up to pull a bottle and some glasses out of the cupboard. He poured them each a shot of whisky and began the seduction.

* * * *

The water ran over Rue's aching body. He braced his hands against the wall and he let his head hang. He banged his fist against the tiles.

"What a fucking waste of time."

Rue grabbed the soap and started to scrub the sweat off his skin. He should have known Vlatko wouldn't have told Stargazer anything. The man didn't even know what he was delivering to Vlatko.

"Did Stargazer tell you anything?"

Rue whirled to see Vlatko leaning against the door frame, arms folded and a quizzical look on his face.

"No." Rue frowned. "I was an idiot to think you'd be stupid enough to tell him anything."

"Ah, maybe, but you've made his year." A smile appeared and Vlatko began to strip slowly.

Rue turned to face the man. "You're okay with what I did?"

Shrugging, Vlatko stepped out of his pants and joined Rue in the shower. "I'm not surprised you did it. Take advantage of every opportunity presented to you. If I was as pretty as you, I'd use what the gods had given me."

"You're not pretty. You're fucking gorgeous." Rue wrapped his hand around the back of Vlatko's head and brought the man's mouth down to his.

Rue nibbled along Vlatko's bottom lip. He tangled his hand in his dark hair. The bells and beads at the ends of Vlatko's braids chimed as they hit together. Vlatko cupped his ass, squeezing.

Rue grimaced and pulled back a little. Chuckling, Vlatko stroked his palms over Rue's sore muscles.

"Stargazer is a little rough."

"You could have warned me." Rue pinched Vlatko's ass to give him a taste of pain.

"Now how was I supposed to know you'd actually seduce the man?" Vlatko licked a drop of water off Rue's shoulder.

"Hey, when I put my mind to it, I can seduce anyone." Rue leant back enough to allow Vlatko more skin to lick.

"Oh, I don't doubt your ability. I just thought I scared Stargazer enough for him to leave you alone. You're a prize worth risking his life for, I guess." Vlatko flicked Rue's nipple with the tip of his tongue.

"You're not going to kill him." Rue groaned as heat rushed through him.

"Mmm..." Vlatko didn't answer him.

"Fuck." Rue arched, thrusting his cock through Vlatko's calloused palm as the man stroked him.

Vlatko left Rue's right nipple alone for a second to shoot him a grin. "That's what I'm planning on doing to you."

Rue's eyes rolled and he shivered. His ass was sore from the pounding Stargazer had given him. His cock jerked as he imagined how much pain and pleasure he was going to get when Vlatko fucked him.

"I can't wait."

Vlatko flipped him around so his chest hit the shower tiles. He cried out as Vlatko knelt behind him and spread his ass cheeks. Damn. He jerked when Vlatko's thumb pressed into his hole. It felt fucking huge and he knew Vlatko's cock was going to feel like a tree branch.

"Ah," he cried, jumping as Vlatko pushed his tongue in and teased the sensitive ring of muscles. "Vlatko?"

A hot puff of air danced over the small of his back. "What?"

"Don't stop." He wasn't sure if that was what he'd planned on saying, but those were the only words spilling from his mouth.

"Oh, trust me, I won't." Vlatko tasted his ass with a sharp nip.

Rue moaned. He wondered if Vlatko was going to punish him for what he'd done with Stargazer. For some reason, he couldn't work up the fear to worry about what was going to happen to him. He had the feeling he just might enjoy his punishment.

Vlatko pierced his opening again. Rue braced his hands against the wall and arched his back, urging his lover to take whatever pleasure he wanted. Vlatko slid his thumb in with the second thrust of his tongue and reached around with his other hand to grip Rue's cock.

"Oh." A long low sound tore out of him as Vlatko pumped him hard in time with his tongue. He rocked between the sensations, falling into a rhythm that pushed him to the brink. Just before he went over the edge, Vlatko pulled away from him. He gasped as Vlatko gripped the base of his cock hard enough to delay his climax.

"Not yet, Rue. You're going to feel me in your ass before you get to come." Vlatko replaced his hand with Rue's. "Don't move."

He needed Vlatko to fuck him hard, so he wasn't going to do anything to stop the man from doing it. There was no warning. Vlatko shoved his fat cock into Rue's ass and Rue howled. Pain almost swamped him. He was already sore from the reaming he'd taken from Stargazer, but Vlatko didn't relent. Vlatko wrapped his thick arm around Rue's waist, lifting his feet off the shower floor so Vlatko's cock nailed his gland with every push. He forgot about his hand until Vlatko knocked it away and started jerking him off.

No comprehensible words left his mouth. He couldn't catch his breath—his chest slammed against the wall with each snap of Vlatko's hips. The sound of flesh hitting flesh filled the bathroom and his climax settled into his balls within seconds.

"Did you come when he fucked you? When you sit down tomorrow and your ass is sore, you'll know it was me who caused it, not Stargazer. This pretty ass is mine."

The words Vlatko murmured into his ear threw Rue into the most overwhelming climax he'd ever had. His head fell back, resting on Vlatko's shoulder. He ground his ass into Vlatko's groin as pearly strings of cum shot from his cock to paint the wall in front of him. Vlatko stroked him, encouraging him to spill all of his spunk.

Rue shivered as he came down from the pleasure, leaning back on Vlatko and clenching his inner muscles around Vlatko's cock. Vlatko slid out of him. The water was shut off and he found himself thrown over Vlatko's shoulder as the big man strolled out of the bathroom.

"You didn't come," he pointed out, the words ending in a yelp as Vlatko tossed him onto the bed.

"I'm glad you noticed."

Vlatko draped Rue's legs over his shoulders, exposing the man's puckered hole to his eyes. Something had taken hold of him and he wasn't sure he liked it. All he knew was he had to fuck Rue until he heard Rue call his name. After placing his cock at Rue's opening, he pushed in, stopping only when his balls slapped Rue's ass.

He wrapped his hands around those pale thighs and kept Rue spread, snapping his hips in short, hard thrusts. Rue watched through half-closed eyes. For a second, Vlatko worried Rue might be in pain, but the swelling cock and the flush colouring Rue's skin told him otherwise.

"Gonna make you come again and then I'm going to fuck you so deep, you'll be able to taste me," he said through clenched teeth. "Touch your cock, babe."

Rue grasped his pretty dick, then started working it. Vlatko tried to pay attention to how Rue liked his hand jobs, but he soon got lost in the feel of Rue's ass milking his cock with every retreat Vlatko made. The orange flecks in Rue's eyes made his gaze seem like fire and Vlatko swore the man was hotter than any other person he'd ever fucked.

Sweat slid down his cheek and dropped to Rue's flat stomach, where he almost heard it sizzle when it hit. He leant forward, grabbing a pillow to stuff under Rue's hips to give him a better angle to peg Rue's gland and make the man writhe on the bed. Rue reached up and twisted his free hand into Vlatko's hair, holding tight.

"Vlatko," Rue grunted, his eyes shut tight as his cum bathed their skin. Vlatko kept reaming his ass, enjoying the way Rue's pleasure was causing Rue's inner muscles to contract on his cock.

Vlatko's balls tightened and his climax exploded. He threw his head back, ignoring the grip Rue had on his hair. "Fuck."

He flooded Rue's ass with cum until he could feel it leaking out around his shaft. His hips kept jerking until he was positive Rue had milked him dry. They both moaned as his softened cock slid out. He caught the wince Rue tried to hide when he let Rue's thighs down off his shoulders.

Vlatko crawled out of bed then wove to the bathroom for a cloth. He came back and cleaned Rue off, being gentle with his abused flesh. He washed himself then threw the cloth in the general direction of the bathroom. He climbed back into bed and turned Rue onto his side, snuggling up behind the thief. He nuzzled the sweaty skin at the edge of Rue's blond hair.

"You okay?" he whispered into the man's curls.

"Never better, even though I won't be able to sit down tomorrow." Rue slid his hands over his arms and played with his fingers.

He chuckled. "Try to sleep," Vlatko suggested. "I'm sure it'll help, and I can always rub some lotion on your ass to ease the ache."

"Thanks."

He wasn't sure exactly what Rue was thanking him for but he kept quiet, letting Rue slip into sleep.

* * * *

Vlatko sat under the firebird's tree, gazing up through the leaves to the sky. Vlatko was restless and didn't want to wait around, so he'd gone for a walk. There were times when he hated not being able to sleep.

He was puzzled. Rue seemed to believe he'd be angry with him for seducing Stargazer and if Vlatko were a different person, he would be. But he couldn't shake the feeling that it would be like being angry at a fish for swimming. Rue did what he had to do to survive, and Vlatko couldn't argue with that. He sighed and rubbed his forehead.

He hated thinking about life and emotions. He was a hired killer, for fuck's sake. What did he care about emotions? He didn't need feelings to do his job. It wasn't like he and the thief were committed partners. They had great sex. Did he want more than that? He stared down at his hand. His fingers trembled and he could feel a hint of weakness in the muscles. Shaking his head, he knew he didn't have time for a relationship.

The assassins the IUM created didn't live long. Their expectations in life weren't much. To do their job and have a little fun along the way. They didn't even expect to make friends. And when the end came, they wanted to be alone.

Vlatko had known on his last job that his time was running out. That was why he'd deserted and come to this planet. He'd wanted to find a way to reverse the damage done to him. So far he'd failed and if he didn't figure out the reverse formulas, the IUM wouldn't need to worry about the information he had. He'd be dead.

Rue crashed through the brush and dropped to his knees in front of Vlatko. "I'm sorry."

Vlatko frowned. "Sorry for what?"

"For what I did with Stargazer. I shouldn't have." Rue hung his head.

Vlatko reached out and tilted the slender man's chin so he could see those pretty eyes. "You did what you needed to do to accomplish your goal. Would it make you feel better if I told you I was angry and hurt by what you did?"

Rue shook his head and gave a little grin. "Maybe if you could do it with more conviction, I'd actually believe you." The thief leant forward, kissing him. "For what it's worth, I've never apologised to anyone for what I do."

"I accept your apology for what it's worth." Vlatko embraced Rue, pulling the man onto his lap.

Rue snuggled close and rested his head on Vlatko's shoulder. "Why are you out here? Shouldn't you be hard at work, typing away at your computer?"

"I needed some fresh air." Vlatko shrugged. "I'm beginning to think it doesn't matter how much work I do with my formulas, I won't find an answer in the numbers."

"What answer are you trying to find? Maybe you just need a fresh perspective."

Vlatko wondered if Rue was fishing for information to send to the IUM. A cramp in his arm told him it didn't matter. He was closer to the end than he thought. "The liquid body armour is a good concept, at least on paper. However, once injected into a human body, it begins to break down. Along the way, it contaminates its host and the cells collapse. The one thing the IUM did to help save my life is eating me alive from the inside."

Rue pushed back with a horrified look on his face. "That's fucked up. What about your ability to heal? Doesn't that counteract the destruction of your cells?"

"Up to a certain point it does, but after a while the rate of destabilisation overwhelms the rate of healing and it's only a matter of time before the host is destroyed."

Rue cradled Vlatko's face in his hands. "But you're the host. You're dying. How can you sound so calm?"

"If I was calm about it, I wouldn't have deserted. I wouldn't be on this gods-forsaken planet, doing research on something I can't even begin to understand. There are a hundred things I can accept, Rue, but my death isn't one of them." Vlatko set the thief away from him and rose to his feet.

He walked a few feet away and glared up at the firebird screeching from her nest. The bird never attacked him, and he had to wonder if the animal knew he was already dead. A pair of slender arms wrapped around his waist. Rue's lips brushed his ear.

"I'll save you."

Rue bit his tongue. *I'll save you* — what the hell was he thinking? He'd never thought about doing anything for anyone else. For twenty years of his life, the only one he'd ever cared for was himself. There was something about the man in his arms. Vlatko made Rue happy in a way no one else had in a long time.

"Why?" Vlatko pressed their hands together.

"Why would I want to help save you?" Rue slid his hands down, stroking a slow path over the zipper on Vlatko's pants.

"Yeah." Vlatko chuckled. "And don't tell me it's because you love my cock. I'm sure you can get fucked anywhere in the universe, you don't need to save my ass."

"Ah, but what an ass it is. I know many a man who'd kill for a ride on your cock, but that's not why I'm willing to help you out." Rue shrugged. "To be honest, I can't give you a good answer as to why I'm willing to put my life on the line and find a cure for you."

Vlatko turned in his arms and cupped his chin. Rue gazed up, searching for any sort of clue that Vlatko might care a little for him. Vlatko's eyes shone with acceptance and fondness. Rue figured it was the first time anyone knew the truth of what Rue did for a living and didn't scorn him, though Vlatko didn't have any room to judge.

Rue slipped his hand around the back of Vlatko's head, tangling his fingers in the braids. Brushing a kiss over Vlatko's cheek, he moved closer to the warm large body. He held his lips an inch away from Vlatko's and said, "You see me."

Rue melded their lips together in a soft kiss, stroking and teasing Vlatko with his tongue. He nibbled on Vlatko's lower lip. Rue wrapped his other hand around Vlatko's waist and held on. Vlatko cupped his ass, lifting him up so their groins fit perfectly together. He twined his leg around Vlatko's muscled thigh to get even closer.

Vlatko pushed his hand between them, fumbling with the buttons on Rue's pants. The cool air rushed over his freed cock and he moaned. Warmth encompassed his flesh as Vlatko managed to undo his own zipper and pulled their cocks together. Groaning, Rue allowed his head to drop forward, resting on Vlatko's broad shoulder.

His sensitive cock rubbed over the calluses on Vlatko's palm as he pumped his hips. Vlatko grunted, pushing harder against him. Pleasure raced down Rue's spine to pool at the base, and his balls tightened. Another stroke and this time Vlatko used his thumb to tease Rue's weeping slit.

"Oh shit," Rue cried out as his cum shot from him, coating Vlatko's hand and their stomachs.

Another grunt and more wet warmth bathed their skin. Rue wrapped his arms tight around Vlatko's shoulders. He found himself crushed in Vlatko's embrace with gentle lips worshipping his mouth. He had the oddest urge to say words he'd never said to anyone before and Rue barely stopped himself from blurting them out. There was no way he could feel that way about this stranger he'd met two weeks ago. He didn't believe in love at first sight. He understood lust. It was an emotion that burned bright and fierce, but didn't last long. Love didn't exist, as far as Rue could tell.

"Let's go get cleaned up and have supper." Vlatko swept him up in his arms. "Then we'll talk. Who knows? You just might come up with a solution no one for fifty years has been able to figure out."

Rue snuggled into that strong, warm embrace, silently praying to any god who might be listening. He wanted to find the solution to Vlatko's death sentence. He didn't want this unique man to die.

The firebird screeched behind them. Rue caught the predator's gaze and it nodded its flaming head at him.

* * * *

After cleaning up, Vlatko and Rue cuddled on the couch in the underground chamber. Rue sat on Vlatko's lap with those thin arms wrapped around his shoulders.

"So how old are you?" The thief's question was soft.

"I'm thirty." Vlatko ran his hand up and down Rue's leg, soothing himself as well.

"When did you sign up to serve the IUM?" The tone of Rue's voice suggested the man thought anyone who joined was crazy.

Vlatko shook his head. "I never signed on. Not really. I told you I was created in an IUM lab."

Rue pushed away, his eyes registering a flare of unease. "You're a clone?"

Vlatko shook his head again. "No. The scientists implanted a fertilised egg into one of their female breeders. They took me away from her right after she gave birth to me. I've never seen her."

"That's awful," Rue murmured, running a hand over Vlatko's chest.

"Why?" Vlatko frowned. "Is there something special about her?"

"She gave birth to you. I think that makes her damn special." A bright smile graced Rue's face.

"It wasn't as if she was given a choice, Rue. The IUM's breeding stock is taken from the planets under their umbrella of power. Most are kidnapped and forced into carrying the fertilised eggs. Given the choice, she'd probably have cut me out of her womb and killed me. I was an alien creature living off her body." Vlatko threaded his fingers through Rue's blond curls.

"No mother should feel that way about her child."

Vlatko could hear doubt and pain in Rue's statement. "What about your mother?"

Rue stiffened and tried to climb off Vlatko's lap. He encircled the thief's waist with one arm, holding him to his body. He lifted that pointed chin and forced Rue to meet his gaze.

"You should know by now I'll never judge you, not even by your own actions. Whatever happened to you when you were young was not your fault. Even though I'm motherless, I know she should have protected you." He pressed a soothing kiss over Rue's trembling lips.

Rue nodded. "I'd still like to get up."

Vlatko studied him for a moment then let go. The thief stood, staring down at the floor for a second before he started pacing. Vlatko leant back. He understood this was going to be hard for Rue—he doubted the man talked about his past very often. He wondered why Rue would choose to tell him. Giving his head a mental shake, Vlatko decided it didn't matter. Sometimes a person just had to trust someone.

"My mom named me. She always told me she rued the day she ever slept with my father. She might have said that it was from the moment I was born, I don't know, but I do know that when I was five she dumped me on the street and told me she was done taking care of me." Rue's hands shook and as Vlatko watched, the thief wrapped his arms tight around his waist, as if holding in emotions Rue didn't want to escape.

Vlatko longed to get up, pull that slender body to his and just hold Rue close. "She was a bitch, Rue. She should never have been allowed to have children."

Rue shrugged. "You're right, but I was five, Vlatko. What kind of monster throws a five-year-old out on the street to live? I'm lucky I managed to survive the first hour, much less a day. I learnt how to steal well enough to feed myself. As I got older, I was taught other ways to support myself." A blush tinged Rue's cheeks.

Vlatko could imagine what other things Rue did to make money. The pretty thief would find it easy to sell himself. A single tear rolled from those amber eyes and Vlatko stood, moving to catch the drop on his fingertip.

"Why are you crying?" He snuggled Rue's shivering body tight to his. "Surviving is nothing to be ashamed of. We all do things we know we'll be ashamed of later, but if it comes down to living or dying, there really is no choice."

Rue's eyes flared a deep orange, then he crushed his lips to Vlatko's. It was an apology and a thank you, all in one. When they were both gasping for breath, Rue pulled back.

"By the time I was sixteen, I was pulling off big jobs and making good money, so I stopped doing everything else, focusing on stealing. I'm good at what I do."

It wasn't arrogance or false pride. Vlatko knew Rue was the best, just as Vlatko had been the best killer the IUM had ever created. He swept Rue into his arms and carried him back to the couch.

Rue traced the outline of Vlatko's lips. "I'm glad the IUM tagged me for this job. No matter how it ends, my life will never be the same again."

Vlatko smiled down at Rue and a wave of feeling rushed through him. He didn't know what to call it, but Vlatko knew Rue had come to mean the entire world to him. He cradled Rue's face and kissed him.

Rue kissed Vlatko back with all his pent-up emotion. He hated talking about how his mother had thrown him away on the street. It made him revert to that five-year-old, feeling as if he was worthless. Surviving the first year on his own had been hard, but he'd learnt valuable lessons and figured out just how tough he was.

Vlatko sipped from his mouth as if drinking the finest Tharanon wine. Rue moved, straddling Vlatko's large thighs. They both moaned as their leather-covered cocks rubbed against each other. He rocked, building the friction and heat. He needed Vlatko to take him hard and fast.

"Now." Rue shot to his feet and ripped the buttons open on his pants. Tugging them down, he managed to get them off without falling over.

Vlatko didn't say anything, just got naked. He seemed to understand how Rue was feeling. Vlatko stood, gesturing to Rue. Rue knelt on the couch, pressing his chest to the back of the furniture and offering his ass to the large man.

"Vlatko, I want you now," Rue demanded when Vlatko hesitated.

"I don't want to hurt you, babe. You're still sore from earlier. We need some lube." A rough hand caressed his ass.

Rue trembled. He didn't want to wait. The pain didn't scare him. He'd felt it before. He needed to have Vlatko buried deep in him. Shaking his head, he reached back, trying to grip Vlatko's cock. "You won't. I want you in me now. Don't be gentle."

The hot breath of Vlatko's sigh warmed the nape of Rue's neck. Vlatko teased Rue's hole with his thick fingers, stroking the sensitive ring of muscles. He whimpered and arched his back, trying to get Vlatko to push those fingers in.

"Hush."

Vlatko slid two digits in and he groaned, leaning his forehead down to rest on the cushions. There was some pain, but he breathed and relaxed his body. Soon Vlatko brushed his fingertips over Rue's gland.

"Shit." Pleasure shot through him, overwhelming the pain.

Vlatko worked that spot for a few minutes until Rue was rocking back, fucking himself on Vlatko's fingers. The big man murmured things into Rue's ears, but the thief was slowly becoming lost in passion and lust. It was a shock when Vlatko pulled out, leaving Rue feeling empty.

"No," he protested, his body begging for more.

"Don't worry, darling. I'll take care of you."

He heard Vlatko spit and figured he was covering that wide cock with his own saliva to try to ease its way into Rue. For all the man might have been a cold-blooded killer, he did seem to take care of Rue, even when Rue didn't want him to.

"Ready?"

Vlatko's cock rested at Rue's opening. Rue nodded and pushed back as Vlatko rocked forward. The pain was almost too much to bear. He cried out and Vlatko stopped.

"I knew I should have gotten the lube. Wait a second. I'm going to pull out and get it."

"No." Rue gritted his teeth and clenched his inner muscles. "Just keep going. It'll be all right."

"I'm hurting you." A kiss brushed over the sweaty skin between Rue's shoulder blades. "You're the one person I'd never hurt in this entire fucking universe."

He shook his head. "I've been hurt before."

"Not by me." Vlatko's hands rested on Rue's hips as he started to ease out.

"I need this to hurt, Vlatko. This time it needs to be me making the decision. Whenever it hurt before, it's been because I've had no control over what was happening to me. By allowing you to do this to me, I'm taking power."

"So you're exorcising some demon with me?"

Rue didn't think Vlatko was angry. The man sounded more thoughtful than upset.

"Yes."

"Okay."

Vlatko slammed back in and Rue screamed. In seconds, the pain was taken over by pleasure as Vlatko worked his cock's head over Rue's gland. He knew he would have bruises on his hips from where Vlatko's fingers bit into his flesh. His balls tightened and pleasure pooled at the base of his spine. It wouldn't be long now.

"Vlatko, I'm…"

Vlatko peeled one of his hands off from Rue's hips and fisted his cock in an almost painful grip. Two strokes in rhythm with Vlatko's thrusts. Rue's climax exploded through him. His vision darkened. He heard Vlatko grunt and cum filled his inner channel.

Just before he let the darkness take him, he reached back and stroked a trembling hand over Vlatko's side. "Thank you."

Chapter Six

One week to go

Vlatko heard Rue's shout of triumph from the hallway. A smile crossed his face. The thief must have figured out how to open the fifth room. Vlatko had known the lock wouldn't present too much of a challenge for the slender man. Actually, the lock wasn't meant to keep any determined person out. It was simply meant as a distraction. He chuckled as he thought of the other ways he'd distracted Rue the past three weeks.

"Okay, where do you keep the good stuff?" Rue came stalking out of the hallway to glare at him.

"Good stuff? There's a ton of good things in that room. Didn't you find your little red stone?" Vlatko leant back in his computer chair and grinned at Rue.

Rue pulled the stone out of his pocket and rubbed it between his fingers. "Yes, I did. What kind of gem do you think it is? It doesn't shine like any ruby or garnet I've ever seen." With a casual flick, he tossed the stone to Vlatko.

Vlatko caught it and held it up to the light. The beam shining through the stone fractured into shades varying from orange to red. A stray thought entered his mind and he remembered a mission he'd gone on.

"I don't think this is a ruby or a garnet. It's something much rarer." He set it down on the desk and started typing. A page popped up on a different screen. He rolled his chair over to the monitor. "That's what I thought."

He gestured for Rue to join him. When the thief got close enough, he wrapped his arms around him and pulled him down to sit on his lap. "The Councillor's Heart you stole from the Mitcov delegation is actually a fire opal."

"A fire opal? Really? I've never seen one of those." Rue plucked the gem off the desk and held it up to the light again. Rue's breath hitched as the stone flared. "Look at that, Vlatko. It gleams like fire."

Vlatko nodded. "It reminds me of the bird in the clearing."

"How much do you think this is worth?"

Vlatko could see the credit signs shining in Rue's eyes. He hugged the thief tight. "On the open market, a whole hell of a lot more than the diamond you took out of the Ecofo museum."

Rue pushed back to eye Vlatko. "You're fucking with me. I got over fifty million credits for that diamond."

"One of my missions was to terminate a gems dealer. He was encroaching on the IUM's own trade network. I spent some time with him, talking and learning his routines. His one ambition was to find a fire opal. He said the highest quality fire opals were mined on Earth over a thousand years ago in a country called Brazil. He told me there were people out in the universe who would give you their entire fortune for what you hold in your hand." He brushed a finger over the gem.

"You really killed him because he was taking business away from the IUM?" Rue sent a questioning glance at him. "Seems a little harsh."

Vlatko sighed. "I did it because I was told to do it. I was created to do as I was told, not to think about right and wrong. I'll be honest and say if I weren't dying, I'd probably still be working for them. Death has a way of changing things and opening eyes." He traced the curve of Rue's hip.

"So I could get at least hundred million credits for this thing?" Rue settled deeper into Vlatko's arms, resting his head of shining blond curls on Vlatko's shoulder.

"A private collector would give you that and more if you wanted. You might want to ask yourself how much the Mitcovians would give you for the return of their treasure." Vlatko trailed his hands from Rue's hip down over the man's thigh and back up.

"Do you think Mitcov would be willing to buy it back from me?" Rue tilted his hips, trying to entice Vlatko to stroke the bulge in the front of his pants.

"The rumours I've heard say Mitcov need the Heart to survive. Without it, they're weak. The IUM can move in and take over. Therefore, if you make it to Mitcov without the IUM hunting you down and taking the gem from you, you could make more credits on that sale than anything else you've ever done. You might even have enough to retire on." He gave Rue a sly wink. "Maybe even retire to a nondescript little planet with a boy toy and have sex all day long."

"Mmm… Now that's a plan I could get behind… Or in front of." Rue waved a hand, gesturing to the two of them. "How much would it cost me to keep you as my plaything?"

"We'll have to see how much you get from a buyer." Vlatko nuzzled Rue's neck. "If you head to Mitcov to try and sell the opal there, maybe you can find someone for me."

"I'm only supporting one boy toy. No sharing for me." Rue gave Vlatko more access to his skin. "Who do you want me to find?"

"The scientist who created the liquid armour is a Mitcovian. If I could find him, I might be able to get the effects reversed or halted." Vlatko nibbled on Rue's earlobe, enjoying the little hitch in the thief's breathing.

"I'll remember that when I leave, but right now I've got other things to think about." Rue spun around and straddled Vlatko in his chair, kissing him while tangling his fingers in Vlatko's braids.

Rue wanted nothing but to keep kissing Vlatko. He knew the dark man was distracting him from his goal, but he couldn't make the effort to care. There was something in the way Vlatko touched him as if he were the rarest Venuvian crystal. He pulled back and tugged off his shirt, then made short work of Vlatko's as well. They gasped as their skin pressed against each other — it was as if electricity ran between them.

He moaned into Vlatko's mouth and shivered as Vlatko's calloused fingers ran over his spine and down over the swell of his ass to grasp his thighs, pulling him closer still. Their erections rubbed on each other through their pants. Rue wanted to feel Vlatko's cock brushing his, but he didn't want to lose touch with the man himself. So he continued to rub, rock, kiss and touch, building the pleasure between them until it exploded.

Rue cried out as his back arched and he flooded the front of his pants with cum. Vlatko grunted, holding him tight as the man's climax raced through him. He slumped, counting on Vlatko's strength to hold him.

"Why?" Vlatko's question was soft as if the man didn't want to ask it, but couldn't help it.

"Why what?" Rue's brain wasn't functioning properly at the moment.

"Why are you still here?" Vlatko pushed up from the chair, carrying Rue with an ease the thief had never encountered before. They moved from the living chamber to the bedchamber where Vlatko set him down on his feet then kneeled to start undressing him.

Rue stared down at the dark braids cascading around the man's shoulders. He caressed them, playing with the bells and ribbons Vlatko used to decorate them. His hand rested on the broad shoulder as Vlatko untied his boots and tugged them off. Rue's pants were next and he grimaced at the cool stickiness of his cum drying in the warm air. Vlatko leant forward and wiped him clean with a shirt.

Rue's heart stopped for a second as he saw the dark head resting next to his pale skin. Rue cradled that strong chin in his hand and lifted it so he could gaze into Vlatko's eyes. There was a hint of vulnerability in the black depths he didn't remember seeing before. Until that moment, he hadn't realised how strong and wide the walls were surrounding the killer's heart.

Vlatko frowned and Rue remembered the question. Why was he still there? He knew how to work the communicator—Vlatko had let him use it to contact Sysu so his accountant knew he wasn't dead yet and didn't make off with all his money. There had been a few days when Vlatko had left him alone. He could have requested Sysu send a transport, getting out of there before Vlatko came back. He tried telling himself it was because he hadn't found the files yet and he hated leaving before a job was done.

"Maybe I like it here. No need to hide. No worries about someone hunting me. My very own bodyguard who takes his job very seriously." He ran a thumb over Vlatko's bottom lip.

Something flashed in Vlatko's eyes before the man grinned. "Maybe it's because you want to figure out where I hid the files. Can't let the rumours start that the best thief in the universe failed to steal something."

Vlatko climbed to his feet and stripped quickly. Placing a hand at the small of Rue's back, he escorted him into the shower. Rue flinched as the hot water plunged down, drenching him. Then Vlatko adjusted the showerheads and moved so his large body took the brunt of the water.

Rue arched into the soapy hands massaging his back. "You might be right. My reputation would be shot if someone found out I couldn't steal those files."

His voice said the words, but his heart knew better. He stayed because of the man taking care of him with such gentle attention. He stayed because for the first time in his life, Rue had found someone he needed more than the next adrenaline fix. Someone who touched his heart as well as his body.

* * * *

Later that night

Something drew Vlatko to the clearing where the firebird had her nest. The darkness didn't bother him – he could see as well in the blackness as he could during the day. A step into the clearing and he knew things weren't the same. A person stood under the firebird's tree. He went on guard.

Rue had been curled up in their bed when he'd left. None of the planet's inhabitants would dare to enter the clearing without some sort of offering. It was a woman. She turned, her hair sweeping behind her. Flames of orange, yellow and red flickered around her. She gestured for him to come closer.

"This is a dream, isn't it?" *He moved to kneel in front of her.*

"Why would you think that?" *Her head tilted in a movement he'd seen the firebird make a hundred times.*

"Because I would never imagine you as a human if I was awake."

Her body was covered with veils marked like her feathers. "It's possible, I guess. I like your young friend."

"You would. He bares your mark." *He thought about the birthmark on Rue's back.*

"He does. Strange, I thought I was the last of my kind. But he doesn't know the power living within him." *The expression on her face resembled a frown.* "It is better he never knows. The burden of fire is hard and only those born to the knowledge can use it without being consumed by it."

"Why are you showing yourself to me now? I've lived on this gods-forsaken planet for years and you've never let me know you were more than a bird." *He sat down, careful not to stare directly at her. She blazed like the sun.*

"The time comes when your friend must leave. His journey is not meant to end here. When he leaves, you must decide whether to stay or to go with him." *Her hand hovered over his head and he could feel the heat roll off her.*

"Will I live longer by staying or going?"

A flinch of her shoulders served as a shrug. "I don't know that. My sight is limited by distance and I can't see all that is to come for you and your love."

"My love?" He had never said those words aloud, and certainly not to Rue.

"Your voice may be silent, but your heart is not. Not saying the words won't make it hurt less if something happens to him." She stepped away from the tree, staring up at the bright stars hanging in the night sky. "It has been so long since I came here. My tree was just a sapling then and the people who live here were far more primitive than they are now. I miss my world. I miss my people." Her burning eyes glanced back at him. "I don't think you understand how I feel."

He shook his head. "No. I have no people and no home to miss. He's the first thing I've ever thought of as mine in my entire life." He stood up and joined her out under the stars. "But I do understand feeling alone."

Without warning, she touched his shoulder with her hand. Fiery pain shot through him. She was marking him and his healing capabilities wouldn't stop this from scarring. He fell to his knees, clenching his teeth to stop from crying out, the stench of burning flesh filling his nose. He closed his eyes.

"Now you will never be alone, my guardian. You'll be linked with me no matter where you are in the universe. Go to your love." Her hand disappeared.

"Vlatko?" A cool hand touched his forehead.

He opened his eyes to find himself slumped against the bed. Rue leaned over the side, concern filling that pointed face.

"What the hell happened to you?" Rue's amber eyes studied the burn mark on his shoulder.

"Now I know why I don't sleep. My dreams are too realistic for my taste." He winced as he climbed up on the bed.

Rue helped Vlatko onto the bed then headed to the bathroom to see if he could find anything to use as bandages. Rue wanted to know what the fuck kind of dream left burn marks on bodies. He found a first-aid kit, which he set next to the bed, then went out to the kitchen to get a bowl of warm water and a cloth to clean the wound. Heading back to the bed, he stopped when he saw Vlatko had wrapped his arms around the pillow Rue had been using. The big man had his face buried in it as if trying to breathe in Rue's scent.

"Hey there. I don't want you to have your dreams if you can get injured in them." He gave a shaky smile.

Vlatko rolled over, grimacing as the sheets rubbed against the wound. "I don't normally dream, even when I sleep, but strange things have been happening since you got here."

Rue bit his lip, dipping the cloth into the warm water before cleaning the angry burn. "Maybe I should leave. I'm not stupid. I know I won't find the files unless you want me to." Vlatko started to say something, but Rue placed a finger over his lips to stop him. "We've shared our bodies and maybe there's something more between us, but I don't expect you to hand over anything that could get you killed. The only reason the IUM hasn't come after you is because of the information you have. Even if I have to leave you, I want to know you're still alive in the universe somewhere."

"You'll be leaving soon." Vlatko took Rue's hand and pressed a kiss to the knuckles. "She said you would have to go and I would have to decide whether to go with you or stay here."

"Who said that?" Rue leant down and brushed a kiss over Vlatko's lips before he finished cleaning the wound and bandaged it.

"The firebird. She was a woman in my dream. This might not have been a dream after all." Vlatko touched the bandage and shrugged. "I'll have a scar there for life now."

Rue sat cross-legged on the bed and frowned. "The firebird living in the clearing? The same bird that winked at me?"

Laughter shook Vlatko's body. Rue smiled, but he was surprised when Vlatko curled up with his head in the thief's lap. The position implied a huge amount of trust on the part of the big man. Rue caressed the braids, moving his hands over the uninjured shoulder down the man's back.

"The same one. If I believed in gods, I would think she was one, but I think she's just an alien to this planet, like us." Vlatko sighed, his body relaxing with each stroke of Rue's hand.

"Why did she call you to her?" Rue believed in gods and powerful beings that could ruin his life on a whim. That's why he prayed to any and all of them.

"I don't know. Just to show herself to me, maybe. She's lonely." Vlatko turned his head. "I asked her if my going with you would mean I'd live. She didn't know."

Rue's heart felt like someone was clenching their fist around it. "I think you'll die either way, Vlatko, but imagine what a ride you'd have if you came with me. I can show you things you've never seen before."

"While we're trying to avoid the IUM and you're carrying around a gem worth a planet? Every other thief in the universe will be after you once they figure out where you are. I'm not sure I want that much excitement. I should be spending my time trying to find a way to stop the deterioration." Vlatko closed his eyes.

Rue stared down at the man in his lap. Time slowed and Rue knew he had a decision to make. "Rest." He whispered a kiss over Vlatko's forehead as he eased out of the bed.

"Where are you going?" Vlatko rested his head on Rue's pillow.

"I need to think. I can't do it here. You're too distracting and I need to have a clear head for what I'm going to do." Rue waved and headed out of the underground chamber. He knew where he had to go.

Rue returned to the clearing where Vlatko had found him and, like Vlatko, he found a woman instead of a bird. She reached a hand out to him and he knew somehow this meeting would be the most important one of his life.

* * * *

Vlatko lay on the bed after Rue had left. He wasn't tired. His body had got its quota of sleep for the week. He stared up at the ceiling and thought about all the work he'd done while living on this planet. Did he want to jeopardise all of it by leaving with Rue? But, truly, what would he lose? He was going to die anyway. What did it matter if he died alone on this primitive planet or went on the ride of his life with the thief?

He climbed out of bed and headed to his computers. He had another week before his deadline for Rue was up. Then the thief would have the option of calling the IUM or leaving with the Mitcovian gem and making a deal with some collector. Vlatko rubbed his finger over the Councillor's Heart Rue had left sitting on Vlatko's desk. Odd warmth traced up his arm and stopped at the spot where the firebird had burned him. Maybe he had an infection setting in, but that would be impossible. His genetic makeup wouldn't allow him to get sick.

Shrugging the strange occurrence off, he booted up the computers and started working. Somewhere in the formula for the armour was the answer to his dilemma. He wasn't smart enough to understand the numbers and code. He needed the original scientist who'd created it. He often found himself wondering if the man knew what his creation would do to the men it was injected into. Or had the IUM stolen it from him to use without caring about the consequences? That scenario was the one he believed in.

Vlatko didn't know how much time had gone by when he glanced up to see Rue sitting on the couch, watching him. He gave the slender man a smile. Rue didn't smile back. Those strange amber eyes studied him as if he were a fascinating bug Rue had found.

"Did you figure things out?" He wasn't sure he wanted to hear Rue would be leaving. He knew he was worried the thief would decide to leave now instead of waiting for another week. He didn't want to lose the man.

Vlatko wondered when he'd gone from not needing anyone to loving Rue and all in the space of three weeks. Was it the threat of dying weakening the walls around his heart enough for this thief to sneak in and steal his love?

"Yes. I know what I have to do and I have to admit it's not what I'd ever planned on doing." Rue stood and strolled towards Vlatko.

He watched as Rue knelt down between his legs. Rue's eyes usually flared orange and red when the man was gripped by strong emotions. Vlatko knew this from all the times he'd watched Rue climax. Now they were calm amber, gleaming with a certainty Vlatko had never had the pleasure of feeling.

Rue unbuttoned his pants and pulled his cock out. He drew in a breath when Rue licked his tip, teasing the slit with his tongue. Vlatko reached out and brushed a shaking hand over Rue's blond curls.

"Is this a goodbye present?" He didn't know why he had asked. It would be better not to know Rue had made up his mind to leave.

The smile on Rue's face was a mixture of sadness and happiness. "Not yet. I still have a week left." He swallowed Vlatko down to the base of his shaft.

"Gods," Vlatko groaned. "I'm going to miss this."

Rue pulled off him with a pop. "Who says you have to give this up? You could come with me."

Vlatko chuckled, but didn't say anything.

Rue fought the need to tell Vlatko he wasn't joking. He really did want the man to go with him, but he wasn't going to beg. The decision had to be Vlatko's. Rue knew there was no way he'd forget about the killer. His mission had been rearranged the moment the IUM had left him on this planet and he wasn't going to complain about it. For the first time, he was important to someone as a person, and not just for a fuck or a paycheque.

He licked his way up the throbbing vein on the underside of Vlatko's cock. Swirling his tongue around the crown, he tasted the pre-cum leaking from the slit. He slipped one hand down to fondle Vlatko's balls, squeezing gently. He wrapped his other hand at the base of Vlatko's shaft then sucked him down.

"Fuck." Vlatko arched off the chair, thrusting deep into Rue's mouth.

Rue relaxed his muscles and allowed the head to hit the back of his throat. As he pulled off, he slid his hand up. The rhythm he established included rolling Vlatko's balls in his hand. He gave Vlatko a light nibble at the crown, then went down on him again.

Vlatko threaded his hands through his hair, holding Rue still as he started fucking his mouth. Rue usually hated when his trick did that, but Vlatko wasn't a trick. He was someone Rue was more than willing to give up control for. He let go of Vlatko's body and braced himself against the chair, letting the big man use him as he wanted.

The thighs bracketing him tightened and he knew Vlatko was close. Rue hummed and the vibration caused Vlatko to moan.

He nodded, encouraging Vlatko to give him what he needed. Vlatko yelled and spurts of cum flooded Rue's mouth. The thief drank down Vlatko's seed as if the bitter-saltiness was the finest wine. He swallowed until Vlatko relaxed back into the chair. Vlatko held him so tightly, then stroked his hair with a light touch.

Rue licked the softening shaft clean then rested his cheek against Vlatko's thigh. Vlatko smiled down at him, tracing his rough, calloused fingers over his eyebrows and down along the line of his jaw.

"I do believe you're the best thing to fall from the sky in a long time." Vlatko's voice was low and satisfied.

"I didn't fall. I was left here to seduce you into telling me all your secrets." He tucked Vlatko's cock back into his pants and zipped them up.

Vlatko lifted him into his lap and Rue curled up, wrapping his arms around the killer's neck. He nuzzled close, laying his head on Vlatko's chest, listening to the heartbeat.

"Are you needing?" Vlatko's large hand cupped his cock.

Rue shook his head. "No, I came when you did."

"Seems to be a habit of yours. You'll want to clean up." Vlatko surged to his feet, not even hesitating at Rue's weight. "You have seduced me, thief. And all my secrets are yours."

"Not all of them. I still don't know where your files are." Rue winked, trying to let Vlatko know he wasn't too worried about not finding them.

Vlatko stripped him and placed him in the shower. He leaned against the wall, watching Vlatko pull his own clothes off. The shower came on and Vlatko blocked the water from drowning Rue.

"The files are in my head." Vlatko soaped up his hands and started massaging Rue's chest.

"You memorised them?" Rue closed his eyes, moaning at the pleasure caused by those hands.

"Yes and no. I do know what they all say, but I had a small chip implanted at the base of my skull. It holds all the files."

Rue's eyes popped open. Vlatko was staring at the soap bubbles coating Rue's skin. "So there was no way I would have ever found them. Why did you tell me I had four weeks to search for them if you knew I'd never discover where they were?"

Vlatko's dark eyes met his and he saw the vulnerable need shining in them. "Because I wanted you to stay."

Chapter Seven

The next day

Vlatko stared at the computer screen. He was still reeling from admitting to Rue that he wanted the thief to stay. Obviously the man's blow job had turned his brain to mush and switched off some vital connection between his thoughts and his tongue. The numbers in the formula blurred and he shook his head. Who would have known his life would take such a turn when he found a naked man tied to a tree three weeks ago?

Rue came up behind him, grasping his shoulders and massaging. Fluid warmth moved through Vlatko's body. He'd noticed the heat the night before when Rue had touched him.

"Rue, what did the firebird say when you went to see her last night?" Vlatko let his head fall forward, allowing Rue to work his neck muscles.

"Something about my hands being good for you and my touch making you happy." Rue brushed Vlatko's nape with his kips.

He laughed. "She's right. What else did she say?"

"You need to burn in the fire and rise from the ashes. It's the only way you'll be healed." He felt the thief's hands tighten on his shoulders.

"I don't think she meant literally. I'm pretty indestructible but I'm not fire-resistant." Vlatko swivelled the chair, causing Rue to jump out of the way. "Let's go soak in the hot springs."

"Does heat help you?" Rue followed him up the ladder into the hut.

"Yeah, it does. I noticed your hands seem warmer than usual since last night. Did she touch you?" He stripped and set his clothes on a stone nearby.

"Took a hold of my hand and said the truth of my past was gone, but I could choose the path my future took by trusting my own decisions. While she was talking, it felt like my hand was on fire."

Vlatko watched Rue shed his clothes then helped the naked man into the pool. He sat down on the carved stone ledge, settling Rue next to him.

"You've made a decision." Vlatko couldn't decide whether he was happy or not.

"Yes. I'll have you know it was a difficult one. I've never done anything like this before." Rue's amber eyes were serious.

"So you're not going to give the stone to the IUM?"

Rue shook his head, his blond curls bouncing as the steam tightened them. "That was never an option the minute you told me they were using me."

"So what are you going to do? Sell the stone on the open market?" Vlatko leaned his head back and relaxed, letting the heat soak into his body.

"No, I'm going to Mitcov."

Vlatko stiffened next to him.

Rue sat back a little to look up into Vlatko's dark eyes. Vlatko was staring down at him in confusion.

"You're going to offer to sell the Councillor's Heart back to them at a substantial profit, huh?"

He could tell Vlatko didn't know why he'd go back to the stone's owners unless it was to make more money than he'd ever see in his life. He shook his head. "No. I don't really need any more money. Hell, I've got more than enough to buy a small planet."

"So if you aren't selling it back to them, what are you doing? You know the IUM will be waiting for you to leave this planet. They'll try to take you and the stone."

The concern in Vlatko's voice warmed him. "I'm not worried about the IUM. If I can borrow your communicator, I'll work out a diversion with Sysu and they'll think I've already gotten off the planet."

"If you don't want the money, why are you doing this? Why risk everything by going there?"

Rue played with the water as he mumbled, "I'm doing it for you."

"For me?" Vlatko slid his blunt finger under his chin and lifted it so their gazes could meet. "You'll risk getting caught by the IUM? They'd throw you in prison or worse. You'd put your life in danger for a killer like me? Why? I'm not that good a fuck."

Rue frowned. "It's not about the sex. Though that's been awesome. It has to do with the fact that when you look at me, you don't see another pretty boy whose body you can use for a few credits. Or as an annoying thief you'd love to get rid of." He cradled Vlatko's face in his hands and smiled. "You see me with all my faults and lies. You've seen behind the walls and still like me. I don't want to let you go."

Vlatko kissed him. Their lips met in the sweetest kiss Rue had ever known. It was flavoured with caring and tenderness along with some strange emotion he'd never felt before. The big man grasped his waist and pulled him until he straddled Vlatko's thighs.

Vlatko rested his forehead against Rue's. The thief saw happiness fill those dark eyes.

"I love you," Vlatko whispered.

Vlatko could feel the shock of the words as they registered in Rue's brain.

"You-you love me?" The usually composed and confident man stuttered.

"I think so."

"You think so. What the hell kind of answer is that?" Rue pushed back so he could see his face, but didn't climb off his lap.

"Hell, Rue, I don't know what love is, but it has to be what I'm feeling." He stared at Rue's amber eyes and traced the cute button nose with his finger. "I don't want to be anywhere except close to you. Your scent turns me on now, but like you said it's more than just the sex. It's about being with someone who understands without needing the words."

Rue threaded his hands through Vlatko's braids and jerked his head forward. This kiss wasn't gentle. It was rough and hard with teeth and tongues. Vlatko slid the slender thief closer to him so their cocks rubbed together. He let Rue stay in control of the kiss while he wrapped both cocks in his hand and started stroking.

"Damn." Rue bit his bottom lip before throwing his head back and thrusting.

He chuckled. "That's it, love. Fuck my hand. Feel my cock rub against yours. I've got you." He teased Rue's crease with his other hand, playing with Rue's sensitive opening.

"Oh." Rue's eyes closed and his back arched. He was the perfect picture of wanton pleasure.

"I've got you. Just let go." He could feel his own climax building. It was only going to be a matter of seconds now. "Come with me, Rue."

As the first spurt of cum shot from his cock, Vlatko thrust his finger into Rue's ass and nailed the man's prostate.

"Fuck." Rue's cum mingled with his in the water.

He continued moving his hand, encouraging every last drop from them both. When Rue slumped over, resting his head on Vlatko's chest, Vlatko eased his hands around Rue's waist and held him close.

"What do we do now?" Rue murmured.

Vlatko laughed. "Right now, we go take a nap."

"Sounds good to me."

"Hold on tight." Vlatko cupped Rue's ass and stood, waiting for Rue to wrap his arms and legs around him before he climbed out of the pool.

He didn't worry about their clothes, just stumbled into the hut and flopped down on the cot. Rue sprawled over him, creating a blanket with his own body. Vlatko didn't want the thief to get cold, so he found a sheet to tug over both of them.

Even his body agreed a nap was a good idea. He set his internal alarm clock. They had a lot of things to work out.

* * * *

A few hours later

Rue shifted, slowly coming awake. His eyes took in the stone above him. He turned his head and saw he was in Vlatko's bedroom underground. How did he get down here? The last thing he remembered was lying on top of Vlatko up in the hut. Vlatko must have brought him here when the big guy woke up.

A jolt of surprise raced through him when he remembered what Vlatko had said to him. *Shit.* He sat up and turned, dangling his legs over the edge of the bed. Did Vlatko mean it or was it just the sex talking? Damn—when had he become such a girl? It didn't matter at the moment whether he'd meant it or not, he had said those words and that was enough for now. Even if Vlatko didn't love him, it wouldn't change his decision. He was going to Mitcov. He got up, cleaned up and headed out to the main room.

Vlatko was talking on the communicator. "Thanks, Stargazer. I'll see you the day after tomorrow."

"What were you talking to him for?" Rue still felt guilty for having sex with Stargazer, even though before Vlatko, he had done whatever he had to do to successfully complete a job.

Vlatko stood and went to the kitchen, pulling out two ales. Rue caught the one thrown at him.

"He's dropping off a transport we can use to make a run to Mitcov." Vlatko popped the top off the bottle and took a swig.

"You're going with me?" Rue asked, a little surprised.

"Yeah. Don't you want me?"

"Sure. I thought you'd want to stay here. There's no guarantee what I'm going to try will even work." He fiddled with the label on his bottle.

"I don't know what your plan is, Rue, but I see it this way. I can stay here, pound my head against this formula and die or I can go with you and have a great adventure—not to mention incredible sex—and die. Either way I'm dead. I decided I want to have fun before this stuff takes me out."

Rue blinked back the moisture in his eyes and coughed. "Okay. I could always use back-up."

"I'm good at that." Vlatko grabbed his hand and dragged him over to the couch. "Tell me what your plan is."

"I'm going to negotiate with the Mitcovians. I'll give them back their stone if they give me the scientist who invented the armour. I figure we could bring him back here and get him to find a cure for you."

"You think that's going to work? We don't even know if the Mitcovian is still alive."

Vlatko hadn't shot his idea down, so it might have the possibility of working.

"Well, Mitcovians live a long time. It's possible he's alive. Why wouldn't they do it? If the fire opal keeps them strong and safe from the IUM, why wouldn't they give up one puny scientist? It's not like we're going to kill him. We're just borrowing him for a few months."

Vlatko chuckled, urging Rue to sit closer to him. "You wouldn't object to being sent to some strange planet with a thief and an assassin?"

Rue nodded. "You've got a point. We could kidnap him. I mean I'm good at stealing things. Usually inanimate objects, but still, how hard could it be?" At Vlatko's sceptical snort, he grimaced. "You're right. It's a bad idea, but it was the only one I could think of."

"Hush, love. I didn't say it was a bad idea. We'll give it a go. If it doesn't work out, we'll think of something else. Maybe we should just fly off together, sell the stone and make a shit-load of credits. We can live the good life while dodging the IUM." Vlatko playfully pinched Rue's cheek. "I always thought I deserved the best."

"I don't want you to die, Vlatko. I hate the idea of your life being snuffed out." He felt his bottom lip tremble. "Aren't you afraid to die?"

"No, I never was. If I had never met you and died, it wouldn't have been a terrible hardship. I didn't have a life. Now since I've met you, the thought of dying makes me angry. I don't want to give you up."

Rue nestled close to his lover's warm body. He traced his hand over Vlatko's thigh. His skin began to tingle and Vlatko gasped.

"Can you feel that?"

Rue shook his head. "All I feel is a tingle. What are you feeling?"

"It's almost like my leg is on fire."

He started to pull his hand away. "I'm sorry."

"No. Keep it there. My leg's been bothering me for a couple of days now. Your touch is making it feel better." Vlatko brushed a kiss over Rue's forehead. "Guess I'll keep you around after all."

Chapter Eight

Two days later

Vlatko sighed as he settled into the co-pilot seat. Rue was going to fly the transport, which made Vlatko happy—he'd never got the hang of steering a ship through the stars. It would be just the two of them on the journey. Stargazer had offered to accompany them, but Vlatko had turned him down. He could see how the mercenary made Rue uncomfortable. Moreover, he didn't want to share the thief. That pretty bubble ass was his.

Rue smiled at him while going through his pre-flight check. "Eager to get off this piece of shit planet?"

"It's not so bad. Maybe not so advanced as other planets, but that's nice sometimes. There's less hassle and intrigue. If they don't like you here, they kill you."

Rue laughed. "That does keep things easy. Now, it'll take us a week to get to Mitcov. We'll have to decide before then how we'll contact them." Rue gestured towards the trapdoor leading down to the entrance of

Vlatko's underground chamber. "Everything locked up?"

"Yes. Here are the codes." He held out a slip of paper to Rue. "If I die, use this place as a bolt hole when things get too hot for you."

Shaking his head, Rue shoved the paper back at him. "The only way I'm coming back here is with you. I don't want those codes."

Vlatko stuck them in his pocket. He'd put them in Rue's bag when the thief wasn't around.

"Once we're headed in the right direction, we can engage the autopilot. I won't need to manually steer until we're closer to Mitcov. There's a dead asteroid I want to use as a staging area."

"What do we do while we're travelling?" He winked at Rue.

"I think we can find something to pass the time with." Rue swept his gaze over Vlatko's body, lingering at his groin.

Vlatko got up and stood behind the pilot's seat. He slid his hands down Rue's chest, stopping to play with the hard nipples thrusting up from underneath Rue's T-shirt. Rue moaned and tilted his head to the side. Those blond curls Vlatko was so fond of cascaded away to reveal the length of Rue's pale neck. Vlatko kissed the sensitive spot right behind Rue's ear, teasing and sucking. Rue's hands stuttered as they checked switches and buttons.

"I don't think this is a good idea." Rue's protest didn't have any heat behind it, since his hips lifted off the seat when Vlatko pinched his nipples.

"Why not? One last time on this planet. Good memories here." Vlatko scraped his teeth over the spot while he tweaked those hard nubs with his fingernails.

"Uh…" Rue seemed to be interested in something other than memories. He reached up behind him and wrapped his arms around Vlatko's neck, causing his body to arch towards Vlatko.

Vlatko couldn't help chuckling. His thief was a slut, no doubt about it. Standing up, he broke Rue's hold on him and spun the pilot's seat around, so Rue was facing him. He pulled the thief to his feet, starting to unbutton his pants.

"Naked." He smiled as Rue rushed to obey the order. "Don't give yourself leather burns getting those pants off, love."

Rue stuck his tongue out at him and he shook his head. "Don't be sticking that out unless you're planning on using it."

Rue's eyes gleamed like fire as the thief fell to his knees in front of Vlatko. Rue flicked his tongue out to lick the top of Vlatko's cock as he got his own pants unbuttoned and pushed out of the way. Those fine blond curls bobbed as Rue swallowed his cock down.

"Those are the memories I love," he growled.

A few minutes later, Vlatko leaned over Rue, bracketing him with his arms as he braced himself on the chair. He didn't want to put all his weight on Rue. He smelt the scent of sex and sweat. With a lazy lick, he tasted the salty drops beaded on Rue's back and traced the outline of Rue's birthmark.

"I'm going to miss her." The random thought skipped off his tongue.

"Hmm…? Who are you going to miss?" Rue didn't lift his forehead from the back of the chair.

Vlatko pressed his lips to the middle of the red mark, waiting for Rue's heartbeat to slow down. "The firebird."

T.A. Chase

"Why would you miss that creature?" Rue shifted slightly.

Both of them moaned as Vlatko slid out of Rue. He patted the tight ass before heading back to the small bathroom to clean up. He grabbed a wet cloth to take care of Rue as well. He sat down in the pilot seat and pulled Rue onto his lap. The blond-haired man curled up, resting his head on Vlatko's shoulder.

"Why would you miss her?" Rue asked again.

"As strange as it may sound, before you showed up, she was the only creature I had much interaction with. I always had the feeling there was more to her than just being a bird." He laughed. "Of course, I was right."

"We need to get moving." Rue didn't make any effort to get off Vlatko's lap.

"I know. Where do you think she came from?" Vlatko ran his fingers through Rue's hair.

Rue shrugged. "I don't know. Does it really matter?" He flicked the switch to get the engines running.

"I guess not." Vlatko was wondering where Rue came from, since the firebird had informed him Rue was like her. He didn't understand how Rue couldn't know what or who he was, but living on the streets as a throwaway didn't lend itself to knowing anything about your past.

"Get in your seat and let's get out of here. The sooner we meet up with the Mitcovians, the sooner we can get you cured."

Vlatko sighed and lifted Rue up, before setting him back down on the chair when he'd moved out of the way. As much as he wanted to find a way to stop the armour from killing him, he found he was reluctant to leave the planet. He took his seat and buckled himself in.

"Let's get it over with, Rue. I want to know one way or the other if something can be done for me."

Rue's amber eyes met his and a determined light flared in them. "We'll find a way to make you better. No matter what I have to do."

Vlatko didn't know if there was a cure, but he did know he wouldn't regret what they were about to do. For the first time in his life, he was happy.

Chapter Nine

The next night

Vlatko sprawled in the pilot's seat with Rue curled up in his lap. He stared at the darkness of space, not really thinking about anything, just enjoying the quiet. He knew once they made contact with the Mitcovians, there wouldn't be a lot of time for peace.

"What was your first time like?" Rue's soft question broke the silence.

"Quick. Messy and not very satisfying." He tightened his arms around Rue's waist.

"I didn't mean the first time you fucked someone. I meant your first kill." Rue pinched his arm.

"Ow. I knew what you meant. It was quick, messy and not very satisfying." He sighed.

"Not very satisfying? What kind of expectations did you have?" Rue managed to sound shocked.

"All I'd heard from my instructors was how cool it was to stalk my target. What an adrenaline rush killing someone was." He shrugged. "I didn't feel anything. I stared down at my target bleeding to death at my feet and I felt empty. No rush of excitement. No pride at a mission accomplished. Not even guilt or sadness at causing this target's death."

"How old were you?" Rue smoothed a hand over Vlatko's naked chest.

"I must have been close to fifteen. I was considered a late bloomer. Didn't achieve the skills the IUM felt I should before then. One day, my commander came in and handed me a gun. He informed me of my target and that this mission was my final exam. If I succeeded, I'd be given more missions. If I failed, I'd be terminated."

"You were so young," Rue murmured, resting his head on Vlatko's shoulder.

"You started picking pockets when you were five. By the time you were ten, you were stealing more expensive trinkets. By sixteen, you were the most infamous thief in the universe. It seems to me you understand about being young."

Vlatko figured Rue would understand better than anyone else. The thief hadn't had a perfect life either.

"I do. I just don't like it. I never killed any of my marks. Not much challenge for me if I did." Rue shifted. A wry chuckle filled the air. "It's silly to feel bad for you, but I guess it's because I like you and I don't like the idea of you being hurt or used."

"Then I won't discuss any of my training with you. It was harsh, but I didn't know any better." He thought about some of his year mates who had never made it out of training.

"And here I thought the streets were the hardest taskmaster."

Vlatko ran his fingers through Rue's fine hair. "Most people would agree with you, but they've never dealt with the IUM. The Security branch of the military is the highest-funded because they spend millions of credits on their trained assassins. That's one of the reasons the IUM hates me. They wasted all those credits on creating and training me." He decided he didn't want to talk about his past anymore. "What about you? You've been stealing since you were five. What makes you so good at what you do?"

"I told you my mother threw me away when I was five. It was steal or die and even as a kid, I wanted to live. Never knew my father. I was skinny and short. The kind of kid it was easy to overlook. I could get into tight places and hide. At first, I just stole food. Then I figured out there were credits to be made if I stole other things and sold them."

Rue pushed out of Vlatko's lap and moved to stare out of a side window. It had been a long time since he'd thought about those desperate days when he was a kid. Even with all the credits he had now, he still had moments of worry stemming from those days.

"We can find something else to talk about, Rue. No need to relive the past."

Vlatko was trying to give him a way out. Rue realised that. "I guess some days the memories are closer than I'd like them to be." He ran his fingers over the brand on his arm.

"How were you caught?"

"By sheer stupidity on my part. I was too cocky and tried to rob the wrong man. He was an undercover IUM agent. He nabbed me and carted me off to jail, but the judge didn't like the idea of throwing me in prison. I was a child and cute. He sentenced me to a branding and then let them throw me back on the street."

"Branding you on the arm wasn't going to stop you from stealing. They should've marked your face." Vlatko pointed out.

"Ah, you noticed the oddness of my punishment. It seems the judge knew a man who could help me take advantage of my cuteness. When the man found me, my wound was infected, so I couldn't stop him. Soon I was turning tricks." Rue's laugh held bitterness. "I couldn't stop stealing, though. I stole from the buyers. The seller would get in trouble for it and would try to blame me. I never had anything to show for it, but somehow the seller always had a little extra credit around."

Vlatko grinned. "I think I'd have liked the younger you."

"I would have stayed far away from you if I'd run into you. The seller couldn't punish me. The only way he kept his business was by taking care of us boys. If he beat me, he'd have gone to prison. Finally, he had to let me go. I was too big a risk for him. It's what I'd intended to happen all along."

Rue stared into the darkness beyond the window. He saw the image of the seller in the glass. He remembered the fear he'd felt when he was ten, then the contempt that had grown as the years had gone by. It was tough being the property of a man Rue knew was not as smart as himself.

Vlatko embraced him and he leant back against Vlatko's chest. The big man accepted his weight without protest. Rue blinked to clear his mind and the image in the window changed. He was framed by Vlatko's body. The assassin's skin gleamed in the low light the dials gave off. Vlatko's dark eyes met his amber ones in the glass and he understood the message. No matter what, Vlatko would be there to guard his back.

"We won't worry about the past anymore. There's too much going on now to freak out about." Vlatko's lips brushed his cheek.

Rue nodded. His lover was right. Four more days and they'd be negotiating for Vlatko's life.

* * * *

Three days later

"What was it like stealing the Rouge diamond?" Vlatko was in the co-pilot seat, his feet resting on the instrument panel in front of him.

Rue was sitting sideways in the pilot's seat, long legs dangling over one of the arms and leaning back against the other. A fond grin lit up the thief's face.

"I have to admit it was the greatest heist of my career. How could it not be? I boosted the biggest, rarest diamond in the universe out from under the best security system invented."

"It couldn't be too great if you found a way around it."

"Oh, but that was the sheer genius of the job. They had protected it from every type of theft known to man or beast, except for the simplest way. I walked in during the day and stole it out from under their noses." Rue laughed.

His joy in the memory of the job made Vlatko smile. It was great how Rue took pride in how he did his job. Quick, clean and as painless as possible. It was his philosophy too, but he wasn't proud to be a killer.

"They were stunned. I was still in the museum when the guards locked it down. Hide in plain sight, I say.

There was no way I could get out. I hid the diamond. Got searched like everyone else. When they were finished and decided the diamond had already been taken out of the museum, I left without incident. Two weeks later, I sold the damn thing to a collector who paid an obscene amount of credits for the privilege of owning it." Rue's smile disappeared and he gave a wistful sigh. Vlatko reached over, tapping Rue's knee.

"What's wrong, love?"

"I'm going to miss the jobs."

He frowned. "Miss them? What'd you mean?"

"After we get you cured, I don't think I should be risking it. The next time I get caught, it's death. I'm too big a name for the IUM to slap on the hand and let go." Rue gave him a wink. "I don't seem to need the thrill anymore."

"Got something else making your pulse race?" Vlatko leant farther over and stroked Rue's thigh.

"Mmm...yeah, I do and it's a lot healthier for me." Rue shifted, his movements encouraging Vlatko to keep touching.

"You don't seem to be getting a lot of sleep, though. Something's keeping you up at night." Vlatko slid from his seat and knelt next to Rue.

The thief swung around until his legs were resting on either side of Vlatko. "Must be the aches I'm feeling." Rue ran a hand over Vlatko's braids.

"What aches, baby?" Vlatko moved his hands up to Rue's waist and tugged.

Rue came out of the chair and landed on top of him on the floor.

"So many things I don't even know where to begin," Rue whispered against his lips.

"Well then, I'll have to ease them all." Vlatko kissed Rue, taking his time. He needed the taste of the man in his arms and the feel of Rue's body pressed to his.

Chapter Ten

One day later

Rue concentrated on the delicate process of anchoring the transport to the asteroid. So far, nothing had gone wrong on their trip. They'd managed to escape the eagle eyes of the IUM and he'd got them to Mitcov, even with all the distractions Vlatko had thrown at him.

He felt a gentle bump as contact was made. The anchoring lines attached themselves and he shut off the engines. Vlatko gripped his shoulders and rubbed.

"Good flying, love."

Rue ducked his head to hide his smile. He thought the pet names were cute and sweet.

"Thanks." He stretched and stood. "I guess I should clean up before we try to contact them."

He turned and his mouth dropped open. He'd never seen Vlatko in his work clothes. The big man wore leather pants that moulded to every inch of his lower body. Black military boots enclosed his feet. A sleeveless black T-shirt covered that magnificent chest.

The fabric flowed oddly and the light gleamed off it in a strange angle. He reached out to touch it. A cool metallic texture met his fingers. He frowned.

"What is this stuff?" He ignored the holster holding a 3.30 laser handgun.

"It's fabric Kevlar. Strong enough to stop a bullet and a knife. Somehow, the scientists have figured out how to get it to recognise what's attacking me, because if it's a laser, the atoms in the fabric will swell and bind to stop that as well." Vlatko shrugged.

Rue tested the strength of the fabric by grasping the collar in both hands and trying to tear it. The fabric resisted and he grunted. "Shit. Are the pants made out of the same stuff?"

"It's a combination of leather and Kevlar. I'm not crazy like some of the assassins. They trust the liquid body armour so much they don't wear any protection." Vlatko shook his head and laughed. "I'm not that trusting."

"Probably a good idea." Rue stepped back to watch Vlatko slip a vest over the shirt. "What's that?"

"A body vest. Just another form of protection. I have one for you when we go to meet with them face to face." Vlatko held one out to him.

He shook his head. "I'm not going to wear that. I'm a thief, Vlatko. I don't wear Kevlar or carry weapons."

"You won't have to carry any weapons. That's what I'm here for. I'll be the muscle." Vlatko stopped his protest. "It's what I'm good at, love, but I don't want to take a chance you might get hurt. The Mitcovians aren't going to be very happy to see us."

Rue thought about arguing, but there was something in the expression on Vlatko's face telling him the big man wasn't going to listen to him. He took it and bit back a gasp of surprise when he realised how lightweight the thing was. "Are you sure this is going to protect me?"

Vlatko sealed up his own and smiled at him. "It'll stop anything short of a rocket blast. Go on. Get cleaned up and changed. Then we'll see about contacting them."

He frowned. "Now that we're here, I'm not sure how to go about getting in touch with the right people."

"Don't worry. I'll get us in. Just think about what you're going to say to convince them to hand over one of their people for the stone." Vlatko pushed him towards the living quarters, slapping his ass as he went by.

"Shit." Rue realised Vlatko was right. He'd have to do some smooth talking to make the Mitcovians willing to trade with him. He started running reasons through his mind.

Vlatko watched Rue walk away. He shook his head and laughed. He was flattered at how seriously Rue was taking this whole adventure, but he couldn't bring himself to hope. He loved the skinny thief with all his heart and didn't want to die before he got to spend most of his life with him. Yet he didn't believe in miracles, and that was what they needed to keep his body from self-destructing.

He went to the communications link and punched in the code Stargazer had given him. His associate had promised the transporter came with a cloaking device that would hide the ship from Mitcov and IUM radars. Also, he'd given him the name of a person in Mitcovian security to get in touch with.

A chime rang, signalling the communication link had connected with Mitcovian systems. He typed in a name and password, then settled in the seat and waited for a person to appear on the vid screen.

"Who the hell are you and how did you get this number?" A large Mitcovian glared at him from the screen.

He didn't blink. It was the first time he'd seen a Mitcovian, but he'd known what to expect. The Mitcovian male was enormous, scaly and blue. It was a vibrant blue, as if the male's skin was made from the most brilliant sapphire.

"Stargazer told me to contact Allaite." Vlatko didn't show any hesitation.

"I'm Allaite and why would Stargazer tell you to get hold of me? I have too many other worries to be bugged by some stranger." Allaite reached out to push the off button.

"Wait. Stargazer knew I have something you need." Vlatko reached into the small pocket on the inside of his vest. He held the Councillor's Heart between his fingers and let Allaite see the stone.

"*Baisha*," Allaite swore. "Where did you get that?"

"It's not important. The thing is, I need you to bring me someone who can make decisions for the government. My partner and I want to see if we can negotiate an outcome that'll make all of us happy." Vlatko twirled the fire opal, enjoying the heat coming from the gem. It was almost as warm as Rue's hands.

"Your partner wouldn't be the little *baisha* who stole it from us? Does he realise how much trouble he's caused by his actions?"

He snorted. "He's a thief, Allaite. Do you really think he cares?" Vlatko leant forward, focusing on the Mitcovian. "Listen. The IUM set him up. He didn't know what he'd stolen until I told him. Now he's willing to make a trade."

"A trade? Who does he think he is?" Allaite growled.

"Yes, a trade. He could have sold the damn thing or even given it to the IUM. Instead he's coming to you. Bring me someone who can make decisions and meet me here in ten minutes." He closed the link and leant back.

"Will he do it?" Rue joined him.

"Yes." Vlatko turned to see Rue had dressed in black leather pants and a long-sleeved green shirt that fitted him like a glove.

"Where's your vest?" He glared at Rue.

"It's over there. I don't need to put it on until we get ready to meet them. I should be safe in our ship." Rue reached out to touch the gem.

"Fine, but remember to put it on when we leave the ship." Vlatko grabbed Rue's wrist and jerked the man onto his lap.

Rue frowned at him. "If I have to. How did you know who to contact and how to get a hold of them?" He took the fire opal in his grasp. The gem flared as if a flame burned in it.

"Yes, you have to. Stargazer gave me the information. He also made sure the transport came equipped with a cloaking device. Neither the Mitcovians nor the IUM will be able to find us unless we want them to." Vlatko spun them around so he could point to a green button on the far wall.

"I see he thinks of everything." Rue settled in. "I'll do all the talking when the negotiations get started. No offence, but I'm not sure being subtle or even nice is your strong suit."

"No. I'm the strong silent type. I'm going as your bodyguard and back-up. I'll keep the gem on me until you're ready to turn it over." Vlatko sounded as if he anticipated Rue arguing with him.

"Why?" He stroked a finger over Vlatko's nose.

"It'll be harder to take the Heart from me than from you. Even with the vest, you're vulnerable. I don't have any weaknesses." Vlatko bit the tip of Rue's finger. "Except for you. I don't plan on giving them the opportunity to use you."

"I'm glad to know you won't feed me to the wolves." He moaned as Vlatko teased the pad of his finger.

"The only person who gets you or your body is me." Vlatko sucked Rue's finger deep.

"Fuck." Rue groaned.

"I'd love to do more to you, but they're going to be contacting us soon. Do you want to talk to Allaite or just to the person he brings us?" Vlatko set Rue on his feet.

Rue stuck his tongue out at the other man. "You talk to Allaite. He's your contact. I'll deal with the big guy."

"This is your show, love." Vlatko stood up and leaned against the panel. "He should be back any minute now."

As Vlatko finished talking, there was a chime and Rue felt his shoulders tense. For the first time, someone's life hung on his ability to charm and con. He stepped back to allow Vlatko closer to the screen.

"Allaite?"

"Who else would it be, *baisha*? Where is your partner?" The Mitcovian male glared at them.

"Where is the decision maker? I'm not showing mine if you don't show me yours." Vlatko stood right in front of Rue, so the alien couldn't see him.

Allaite sighed. "I brought High Councillor Zalaigh." The security officer stepped away from the screen to allow the high councillor to take his place.

At the same time, Rue switched places with Vlatko. Rue didn't have any idea what he was going to say. He hoped he could convince the Mitcovian to give them what they needed.

The high councillor was only slightly smaller than Allaite and was a softer blue. He wore a white tunic and pants. Hanging around his neck was a gold medallion. There was an empty space in the middle of the disc and Rue wondered what used to rest there — he figured it was a symbol of the high councillor's office.

"Ah yes. So the envoy from the IUM was right." Zalaigh nodded at him. "Rue Thaday. Who else would have the nerve to steal the Councillor's Heart?"

"Sir," Rue kept a respectful tone to his words.

Vlatko wasn't surprised by Rue's tone. Something about the high councillor commanded respect. Vlatko made sure to stand in the shadows behind Rue. He didn't want to seem like he was forcing the thief to talk to the Mitcovians.

"Are you here to beg forgiveness and return my planet's most precious treasure?" Zalaigh's tone was sceptical.

"No, sir. First, I'd like to state that I didn't know the stone I took was yours until my partner informed me. I was hired for a different job and was told the theft of the stone would be my cover." Rue's explanation was basic, but unapologetic.

"We're supposed to believe the word of a thief?" Allaite interrupted.

Zalaigh held up a hand and stopped the other Mitcovian's outburst. "It matters very little why you chose to steal our stone. How much do you want from us for the return of the Heart?"

Rue shrugged and Vlatko could tell his lover was uncomfortable with the conversation. He touched Rue's back, letting the man know he was right there with him.

"If I wanted credits, High Councillor, I would have screwed you all and sold the stone on the open market. I've been told I could get a fortune for it. I'm not interested in fortunes."

"You're not? Strange declaration from a man who steals for a living." Allaite frowned.

Rue gave the security officer a cold stare and Vlatko felt a swell of pride. He knew Rue had always relied on his charm and looks to get what he wanted, but Rue was smart enough to know that wasn't going to work with the Mitcovians.

"I'm here to discuss a suitable trade with your high councillor, not some pumped-up security guard. Keep interrupting our conversation and the Councillor's Heart will disappear into someone's private collection. You'll become slaves to the IUM."

Vlatko wanted to cheer. He knew the Mitcovians admired confidence and strength. Rue was showing both by confronting Allaite.

"Allaite, shut up. Mr Thaday knows he's put us in a position of weakness. We have nothing to negotiate with while he has the gem and the presence of the IUM looming behind him."

"Nothing I do has the sanction of the IUM." Rue laughed. "Trust me. I'm on their hit list by now."

"Right and that's why you have one of their trained assassins standing behind you."

Rue shot Vlatko a glance. He didn't say a word. This was Rue's show. How the thief described his presence didn't really matter to him.

"He no longer works for the IUM."

"No one quits the IUM—especially not their Security branch." Allaite sputtered.

"They do if they have information the IUM doesn't want made public." Vlatko spoke up, keeping his voice low and unemotional.

Zalaigh chuckled. "They must hate you."

"I won't be getting a Naming Day card from them." He moved back into the shadows.

Rue shook his head. "Let's get back on track. We have the stone and we're willing to make a trade with you."

For a second he heard his mind yelling at him, telling him he was crazy to give up all those credits for a man. He met Vlatko's dark gaze. Maybe it was the craziest thing he'd ever done, but it might end up being the best if it worked out.

"What do we have that you could possibly want?" Zalaigh crossed his arms and glared at him through the vid screen.

"We want the Mitcovian scientist who created the liquid body armour the IUM uses." Rue swallowed. This was when they laughed at him.

"What? Oh hell no, *baisha*. We won't give him to you." Allaite exploded.

Rue shot a puzzled glance at Vlatko. The assassin frowned and shrugged.

"Allaite, calm down." Zalaigh wore a confused expression. "Why do you want him?"

"There's something wrong with the body armour. Its atomic structure begins to break down and eventually destroys the body from the inside out." Rue tried to remember what Vlatko had told him. "The person it's injected into has a life expectancy of forty years maximum before their bodies can no longer sustain the damage done."

"Why should we care about their trained killers? If they die, it's one less danger to us." Zalaigh pointed out.

"You're right. I won't argue that point with you. Before I was hired for this last job, I'd have agreed with you." Rue shifted, not willing to say more than that.

"Something changed your mind." Zalaigh's gaze flickered beyond Rue's shoulder for a second. "Or someone. It's interesting to see a thief such as you brought to such an unfamiliar place like this."

"Do we have a deal or not?" Rue didn't want to waste any more time. Each minute they took discussing the trade was a minute closer to the IUM getting hold of them.

"There's a slight problem. I can't give you the scientist."

Rue's heart dropped. It had been worth a try.

"I can allow you to stay on Mitcov and meet with him to see if he can find a solution."

Allaite looked as if he had swallowed a fish. Rue could tell the security officer was livid about the choice. Zalaigh shook his head to keep the other Mitcovian from protesting.

"We'll discuss it and get back to you, High Councillor. The way I see it, my partner and I don't get anything more than a meeting out of this kind of trade." Rue needed to talk to Vlatko. He was almost desperate enough to take it.

Rue knew Vlatko was in pain, though the assassin never complained. The muscle weakness and headaches were getting worse. The only relief Vlatko got was when he touched him and the warmth from Rue's hands filtered through Vlatko's body.

"I'm prepared to offer you and your partner asylum. You may live on Mitcov for as long as you like. We will protect you and harbour you." Zalaigh's grin was vicious. "Once we have the Heart back, the IUM can't touch us."

"High Councillor, we'll contact you when we've reached a decision." Rue shut the vid down and leant back, stretching the tension out of his spine.

Vlatko massaged his shoulders and he felt the touch of lips on his head. He sighed. They were a step closer to finding a way to keep Vlatko alive.

"What do you think?" Rue asked.

"I think it's the best offer we'll get from them. I didn't sense any sort of leeway from Zalaigh about giving us the scientist. At least the guy's still alive."

"You're right. Do you think they'll keep their word about protecting us?" He shivered.

"The Mitcovians are a brutally honest race. They don't take kindly to lies or cheating. To Mitcovians, breaking a sworn oath is the same as killing a child – it's something they would never do."

"Oh." Rue gasped. "So we get Zalaigh to swear an oath they'll protect us and then we take their offer."

"Yes." Vlatko growled.

Chapter Eleven

Several hours later

Rue shifted, his nerves sparking. He prayed this whole meeting wasn't a trap. Vlatko had explained that if it were a trap, Rue was to escape while Vlatko held the Mitcovians at bay. Rue snorted. Like he was going to abandon Vlatko.

He shifted again, trying to find a comfortable spot for his sore ass. Vlatko had found entertaining ways to keep his mind off the upcoming meeting. His hand touched the bite on his neck. Vlatko's mark, letting the Mitcovians know Rue was taken. He glanced over his shoulder at Vlatko who leaned against the wall behind him. A faint smile graced Vlatko's face and a slight wink made Rue laugh.

Allaite entered first. "High Councillor Zalaigh," he announced.

Rue rose to his feet, keeping his hands by his sides. The high councillor entered and Rue felt small. The Mitcovians towered over him and were even several inches taller than Vlatko. He bowed.

"Mr Thaday, only time will tell if it is a pleasure to meet you face to face." Zalaigh held out an enormous hand.

Rue shook it and nodded. "The jury's still out on you too, sir."

"Please call me Zalaigh." Zalaigh gestured to Vlatko. "Do you have a name?"

"Vlatko." The assassin nodded, but didn't move from the wall.

"Why that name? The IUM doesn't name its assassins. They merely assign numbers." Zalaigh sat in a chair facing Rue.

Rue sat. He didn't know Vlatko wasn't the man's real name. Of course, Thaday wasn't his.

"It had meaning to me." The tone of Vlatko's voice said the topic was closed.

Zalaigh folded his hands in his lap and stared at Rue for a moment. "Allaite says he saw the Councillor's Heart in your partner's possession when he first contacted us. How are we to be sure it's the same stone?"

Rue held his hand out and Vlatko dropped the fire opal on his palm. The instant the gem touched his skin it flared, bathing them all in orange light. "Is this your gem?"

Zalaigh's hands shook as he reached for the opal. "I was afraid we'd never see it again."

Rue closed his fingers around the Heart and handed it back to Vlatko. "Seeing will be all you're doing until we talk to the scientist."

Vlatko tucked the stone under the vest he wore, his dark eyes daring Allaite to try to take it from him.

Allaite made a move towards Vlatko and Rue tensed.

"Allaite, no. He's right. The scientist you seek is me." Zalaigh hid his hands under the table.

"You? That's the reason why you couldn't come with us." Rue frowned. He hated complications and this was a major one.

"Yes. Before I became high councillor, I worked as a research scientist. I was trying to invent or find new ways of protecting troops in the field. The liquid body armour was one of many experiments. I was still in the development phase when the IUM offered my assistant a deal he couldn't refuse. His child's life for my formula. He had no choice, and I place no blame on him."

Rue had figured it had to be something like that. Zalaigh didn't seem the type of guy who'd invent something that would endanger the very people using it.

"Did you know about the formula's breakdown?" Vlatko asked.

Zalaigh nodded. "In a way, yes. I knew there was a fault in the formula. I couldn't keep it stable. The atoms kept breaking down. I never imagined human blood would bind and stabilise it enough to keep the test subject alive for even a few minutes, much less thirty years."

Rue tapped the table with his hand. "Do we have a deal then, High Councillor? You swear to give us asylum and protection here on your planet, and in return we'll give you back your Heart."

"What's to stop us from just taking it right now?" Allaite commented.

"Me." Vlatko moved to stand next to Rue at the table.

Rue's lover stared at the Mitcovian security officer with an 'I dare you' smirk on his face. His hand rested on his belt next to the grip of the handgun. His other hand hung, relaxed, at his side.

"Even you can't stop a unit of Mitcovian guards." Allaite's words acknowledged Vlatko's superior strength against one person.

"No, but I can kill the high councillor before any of you kill me."

Allaite growled, but Zalaigh touched the officer's hand and shook his head.

"I'll give you something else if you swear." Vlatko didn't relax, but his offer told Rue Vlatko wanted to take the deal.

"What are you offering?" Zalaigh studied Vlatko.

"I'm offering all the information I have on the IUM. It includes private internal memos sent between high-level commanders about some of my kills. I have enough shit to topple several planetary governments." Vlatko squeezed Rue's shoulder and smiled down at him.

"I swear on the Councillor's Heart to give you shelter and aid until you die. We will protect you as if you were Mitcovians." Zalaigh pressed his fist to his chest. "My promise is law for every living Mitcovian."

"Good. I guess we need to worry about the dead ones now," Rue joked.

Vlatko glared at Zalaigh. "Who are you that you can make promises binding all Mitcovians?"

Zalaigh stood and towered over him, but he refused to feel intimidated by the Mitcovian.

"I'm High Councillor, supreme ruler of Mitcov. I'm also the Guardian of the Heart."

"You sure as hell aren't the person I stole the stone from." Rue's comment caused a smile to chase across Vlatko's face.

"It seems the IUM's reach is long. They corrupted one of my closest companions. She took the Heart. I don't know where she was headed when you ran into her. Allaite and his men caught up to her minutes after the Heart changed hands."

Allaite touched Zalaigh's back. The security officer's touch seemed to ease the high councillor.

"What happens when we give you back the stone?" Vlatko eased over to block Rue with his body. He didn't think the Mitcovians were interested in killing or hurting them anymore, but he wasn't willing to stake Rue's life on it.

"The reuniting of the Heart and the medallion is a private thing. Allaite will show you to a suite that will be yours for as long as you choose to stay. In the morning, after we have rested, we'll meet and go in search of a cure for you." Zalaigh's voice wavered and he braced himself on the table.

The high councillor was weakening. Vlatko didn't want to chance Zalaigh would get too sick to help him. He tugged the stone from his vest pocket then started to hand it to Zalaigh.

The high councillor shook his head. Nodding to Rue, he said, "Please, let the thief touch it one more time."

Rue's eyes widened, but he reached out with a hesitant hand. Vlatko encouraged him with a smile. If Zalaigh wanted Rue to touch it, Rue would.

A burst of light blinded Vlatko the second Rue's fingers landed on the fire opal. He yanked the stone away when Rue started to fall. He tossed it towards Zalaigh before catching Rue in his arms.

After making sure Rue was okay, he checked to see Allaite holding the high councillor in his own embrace. Zalaigh cradled the Heart in his hands. Vlatko and Allaite exchanged a glance. They understood each other. Their first priority was to their lovers.

"I'll send someone to escort you to your suite." Allaite stalked to the door, carrying Zalaigh.

"Thank you, and I hope he is all right." Vlatko sat down in a chair and grasped Rue to his chest. "What the hell happened?"

Rue pressed the hand that had touched the opal to Vlatko's chest. He gasped. It felt as if Rue was holding a burning ember to his skin, even through his clothes.

"Are you okay? Do we need to treat the burns?" He prised one of his own hands from Rue's body to hold the injured hand to the light.

"No. Aside from the heat, I'm fine." Rue reassured Vlatko.

Remarkably, the thief was telling the truth. Vlatko's close inspection of Rue's hand showed no burns or blisters anywhere.

"What the fuck happened?"

Rue shrugged. "I don't know. I touched the gem and it was as if a wall of fire shot through me. It was the most intense heat I'd ever felt, but I wasn't worried about burning up or anything." Rue shook his head. "You'll think I'm crazy."

"Just tell me," Vlatko commanded Rue.

Rue found he didn't want to talk about it. It was too personal, but Vlatko watched him with patient eyes and Rue knew he'd tell this man anything.

"It was like the fire was burning up old memories. As if it used my past as fuel to make the flames grow higher and burn brighter. It was cleansing." He dropped his gaze, sure Vlatko would laugh. A part of his own mind didn't believe what he'd said.

"Fire is one of the most cleansing of the elements. I've seen a forest engulfed in flame. All the trees turned to ashes and you'd swear there wasn't anything alive afterwards. Within days, you could see green leaves peeking out from the burnt grass. Fire brings new life even while it destroys the old." Vlatko stroked up and down his arms.

Rue rested his head on Vlatko's shoulder, exhaustion sapping his energy. He started to say something, but Vlatko hushed him and he settled, allowing his mind to ease and his thoughts to drift.

He woke up when his head hit something far softer than Vlatko's shoulder. He opened his eyes to stare up at an intricate ceiling. The painted tiles resembled a blazing sun. He turned his head, examining the room. All the fabrics were orange, red or white. He felt as if he were caught in a fire. It comforted him. A movement caught his attention and he looked up to see Vlatko prowling around the room.

Rue enjoyed the fluid strides moving Vlatko's powerful body. He wondered if it was weird that the strength and menace Vlatko exuded not only turned him on, it soothed him as well. Maybe his need for safety stemmed from his years on the street. Vlatko made him feel secure and eased his insecurities.

"What does Vlatko mean?"

His lover's gaze met his and he smiled, encouraging Vlatko to tell him. Curiosity ate at him—he wanted to know why the assassin had chosen that particular name.

"It means to rule in peace. It's a shortened version of an old Earth name, Vladimir." Vlatko seemed embarrassed.

"Why pick it?" Rue stroked his hand over the sheets, trying not to reach out to Vlatko.

"I used to help the IUM rule the universe with fear and pain. I thought it would be more fitting to rename myself something reflecting my new outlook on life, since I'm not going to kill anymore. Or at least no one who doesn't deserve to die." Vlatko checked the windows again.

"Are we locked in?" He pushed up so he could lean against the headboard.

Vlatko looked him over and shook his head. "No. There are only locks on the inside of the doors and windows. They're not worried about us running." Vlatko sat next to him on the bed.

"Why would they be? They have what they want. Now we'll have to see if they'll honour their side of the bargain." He reached out and cupped Vlatko's cheek. "Why don't you lie down with me for a while?"

"I'm not tired," Vlatko commented, wrapping Rue in his arms.

"I am and I sleep better with you holding me." Rue tucked his head under Vlatko's chin and sighed. He wasn't interested in what was going on outside their suite. He only cared about this moment and this man. The rest would take care of itself.

* * * *

Allaite laid Zalaigh down on their bed, worry dancing through his heart. His lover hadn't moved since the whole episode in the conference room. He ran his hand over Zalaigh's face, praying everything would be all right.

"Love, please open your eyes," he whispered.

Zalaigh's eyelids fluttered then those marvellous blue eyes Allaite loved so much opened. Zalaigh frowned. Allaite knew he was having trouble focusing.

"How are you feeling?" He stripped the tunic and pants away from the muscular body he found so attractive, but it wasn't time to get turned on. He pushed his lust away and finished getting Zalaigh comfortable.

"Like I've finished a three day binge on Tharanon wine." Zalaigh unclenched his hands and stared down at the red fire opal. "We're saved, Allaite."

"More importantly, love, you're saved. It was too close this time." He trailed a finger over Zalaigh's lips. "I wish there was some other way to protect Mitcov than to tie you to the Heart."

Zalaigh shrugged. "Maybe there is a way, but it'll take more power than we have." He teased the tip of Allaite's finger with his tongue.

Allaite groaned. "You're not up to playing, Zalaigh. You need to rest and then we'll reunite the stone with the medallion."

His lover sighed. "Unfortunately you're right."

Zalaigh sat back, pulling the covers up over his body and setting the Heart down on the nightstand beside him. "So what do you make of our new allies?"

Allaite stood, resisting the urge to join Zalaigh in bed. "I understand the assassin a little better now. I don't necessarily trust him, especially when it comes to the thief. Vlatko will do what he must to keep Thaday safe, even if it means breaking his promise to us."

"But wouldn't you if it meant my life?" Zalaigh laughed. "I know I couldn't be trusted when it came to you. We all have weaknesses, Allaite, and it just so happens all of ours are the same."

Allaite grabbed a chair to pull it beside the bed. He settled down and grinned at Zalaigh. "Do you think Thaday really is that powerful?"

"You saw what happened when he touched the Heart. There's fire burning deep inside him and we have to help him learn how to harness it. If he doesn't, bad things could happen to him and those around him. Maybe he can help us change the way Mitcov is protected." Zalaigh took Allaite's hand in his and squeezed. "Do you have anything pressing to do?"

"No." Allaite stood, stripping off his clothes. He knew what his lover needed. Zalaigh wanted him to wrap his arms around him and hold him close. They both slept better that way.

"Then come to bed. Our new guests won't be leaving and your lieutenant can take care of any problems." Zalaigh lifted the corner of the blanket for him to slide under.

"I must do as my high councillor commands." He pressed a kiss to Zalaigh's lips and encircled the man's waist with his arms.

"You'll at least obey me in this, if nothing else." Zalaigh laughed.

"Obeying you is doing what my heart wants most."

"Such a charming man you are, when you aren't trying to be intimidating." Zalaigh began to play with Allaite's nipples.

He gasped. "I thought you were too tired to play."

"It seems being this close to you has revived me." Zalaigh bent down and flicked Allaite's hard flesh with his tongue.

Allaite groaned and held Zalaigh's mouth to his chest. This was why he obeyed his high councillor — he obeyed for the touch of the man's mouth and the feel of his body against his.

Chapter Twelve

The next morning

Vlatko tensed as he heard the door to their suite open. He reached out to touch Rue, making sure the thief was next to him. He came in contact with Rue's warm hip and he stroked it. Rue's body stiffened, but he didn't say anything. Rue must have heard the same noise. Vlatko didn't have any weapons in the bed with him, except for his own hands. That would have to be enough if their intruder meant to cause them harm.

The steps got closer to the bed and Vlatko launched himself from the bed, his arm catching the Mitcovian around the throat and bringing him down to the floor. Vlatko didn't check to see who it was. He rolled and pressed his elbow hard against the man's throat, growling down at him.

Allaite had a shocked expression on his face, but a sheepish light in his eyes. The security officer held his hands out to the sides, showing Vlatko he didn't have any weapons. Vlatko grunted, climbing to his feet and offering a hand up to Allaite.

"You should really try knocking first, before Vlatko ends up killing you for real next time." Rue sat up in the bed, blankets pooled around his waist and running his hands through his blond curls.

Vlatko saw the appraising glance Allaite gave Rue. He thumped Allaite in the shoulder. "He's mine."

Allaite chuckled. "I know. You can't stop everyone from looking, though. He is rather a pretty piece."

"Hey, this pretty piece is in the room with you," Rue grumbled.

"Yes, he is and yours is rather pretty as well." Vlatko headed for the shower.

"Speaking of the high councillor, he would like you to join us for breakfast in thirty minutes." Allaite winked at him before heading to the door.

"Ah, wonderful. The showers are big enough for two," Vlatko commented as he continued to the bathroom.

Vlatko held back a laugh as he heard Rue's feet hit the floor to chase after him as he went into the bathroom. He bent over to turn the water on and two slender hands squeezed his ass. He held his moan in, pushing back into those hands. A moist tongue licked over the small of his back. When he remembered the water, he straightened and turned, grabbing Rue's arms and hauling his skinny ass into the shower stall with him.

"We don't have much time, but we can still have a little fun," he whispered into Rue's ear.

Rue whimpered when Vlatko pressed him against the tiles and rocked their hips together. Those amber eyes flared with need and passion. He slid his hand between their bodies, grasping their cocks.

"Please, Vlatko." Rue's mouth met Vlatko's and their tongues fought for dominance.

"Are you needing, love?" Vlatko murmured against Rue's neck after pulling away from their kiss.

"Yes." Rue arched, pushing his cock through Vlatko's hand and stroking Vlatko's shaft at the same time.

"I'll give you what you want." Vlatko started jerking them both off, his movements fast and hard.

He reached his other hand up and pinched Rue's nipples. Rue buried his hands in Vlatko's braids, twisting as Rue grunted and arched his back, begging with his body. Vlatko played with those hard nubs of flesh, flicking and scraping his nails over them. He began tugging on them in time with his strokes on their cocks. His climax moved through his body, pooling at the base of his spine and causing his balls to tighten.

"Come with me, Rue," he ordered as his seed shot from his cock, bathing their bodies in his cum.

"Shit." Rue's cum mixed with his in the water.

He continued to move, drawing their climaxes out until there was nothing left in their erections. He let the softening flesh go and turned Rue so the warm water bathed him. Vlatko picked up the soap, then lathered his hands with bubbles to start washing Rue's flushed skin.

"You take good care of me," Rue stated in a satisfied tone.

"That's my job now." Vlatko rinsed them both before shutting the water off.

After manoeuvring Rue out of the shower, he dried him then pushed him towards the bedroom. "Go get dressed. We have to meet the high councillor for breakfast in ten minutes."

* * * *

Rue finished getting ready then joined Vlatko in the hall where a strange Mitcovian escorted them to the high councillor's chamber. He felt anticipation swell in his body. Today was the day they started searching for a way to save Vlatko and he couldn't wait. He bounced on the balls of his feet, his nerves getting the best of him.

Vlatko took his hand and he calmed down. Words tumbled around in his head, but he fought the urge to babble. He couldn't lose control, not when they'd managed to convince the Mitcovians to help them.

The Mitcovian led them to an open room where Zalaigh and Allaite stood. The two were laughing softly and Allaite's hand rested on Zalaigh's cheek. Zalaigh brushed a kiss over the palm of Allaite's hand. Rue saw Vlatko smile. He leaned on the big man, pressing their linked hands against his stomach.

"They love each other," he whispered to Vlatko.

Vlatko nodded, but didn't respond. He cleared his throat, causing Allaite and Zalaigh to move away from each other and towards the table.

"Forgive us for interrupting, High Councillor. Allaite told us you'd like us to join you for breakfast." Vlatko bowed, tugging Rue with him.

"Yes and please, Vlatko, it's Zalaigh. I prefer not to use my title unless I'm doing something official." Zalaigh gestured for them to sit at the table.

Rue had never seen such an elaborate setting. The table was big enough to seat twenty people, though there were only four plates at one end of the table. The plates and glasses were made of the clearest blue Venuvian crystal he'd ever seen. The silverware was polished to a high shine and he was almost afraid to sit down.

He hovered next to his place until Vlatko pulled his seat out for him and pushed him down into it. He was going to screw something up. He'd never been in a beautiful room like this one. Well, at least not during the daytime when he could stop and check everything out. Usually it was dark and he was running to keep from getting caught. He stared down at his hands, wondering what to do.

"You won't break anything and if you do, we'll replace it." Zalaigh sat across from him with Allaite by his side.

Vlatko sat next to Rue and he squeezed Rue's knee. Rue chuckled. "I'm not used to all this finery, Zalaigh. I'm just a street kid turned thief. The only thing I know to do with this stuff is steal it and sell it."

"I'm sure you could get quite a few credits for this." Zalaigh tapped a plate with his finger. "I'm sorry we have to use the grand dining room. I'm a disappointment to my staff, I'm afraid. I don't get into the trappings of my position."

Allaite signalled for breakfast. The servants brought out plates filled with fruits, eggs, meats and breads. It was all real, not the synthesised crap Rue got on other planets. After their plates were filled, the servants disappeared out of the room and the four men stared at each other.

Rue wondered what they'd talk about. He didn't have friends, so small talk wasn't a tool he knew how to use. Unless he was trying to charm someone out of a trinket.

Vlatko cut a pear and handed him a piece. "You mentioned the IUM envoy when we first talked."

Zalaigh grimaced. "The little weasel arrived on our doorstep shortly after the Heart was stolen. Butter couldn't melt in his mouth as he spoke about helping us find our treasure, and told us the IUM was prepared to do whatever it took to get it back."

"I wanted to wipe the *baisha*'s smug expression off his face. I wish I could be there when he finds out we have the Heart back." Allaite snarled, clenching his hands in anger.

Vlatko shot the Mitcovians a glance. "You mean you haven't told the IUM you have the stone yet?"

Zalaigh shook his head. "No, we haven't. I want to see how long it takes before they figure it out on their own, or make a move. By now, they know you and Rue have disappeared. They'll try to get information from Rue's associate."

Rue laughed. "They can do whatever they like to Sysu. The man won't tell them anything."

Vlatko wasn't sure about that. "The IUM can make people talk. Your friend seems to be the type who'd sing for credits."

"Offer him enough and Sysu would sell you his grandmother. But he won't tell them anything because he doesn't know where we went. As far as he's concerned, I've dropped off the map." Rue took the pear Vlatko had sliced for him and munched with a grin on his face.

"What about all those credits you've made throughout your career?" Allaite ate quickly.

Vlatko noticed Allaite kept an eye on what Zalaigh ate. Was it just taking care of his lover or was Zalaigh weaker than they thought?

"I doctored my accounts. The instant the credits go in to the accounts Sysu has access to, a majority of it funnels out to several other hidden ones. If he or the IUM investigates, all my money's still there, but in reality there's only enough to cover Sysu's percentage." Rue wiggled his eyebrows at Vlatko. "That'll surprise the shit out of the little bastard when he tries to steal my credits."

They laughed, but Vlatko wasn't going to let the subject of the IUM rest. He glanced around the room. "How much trust do you have in your staff?"

Zalaigh's eyes narrowed. "I have complete trust in them now. Allaite handpicked the ones in my inner circle. He deals with any others I might meet. I might not trust them, but I'd trust Allaite with my life."

"Fair enough. I think we should be prepared for the IUM to try something. They aren't known for giving up, even when the odds are stacked against them." Vlatko checked to make sure Rue didn't need anything.

Allaite agreed. "You're right. I have one of my most trusted officers watching the envoy. If he tries anything, Rellam will tell me."

"Things will come to a head when the IUM realises Rue and I are here." Vlatko leant back in his chair, eyeing the high councillor and his chief security officer. "What safety precautions do you have in place? I'll help out. It seems to me protecting you, Zalaigh, is the most important thing, since you're tied to the Heart."

Surprise showed on Rue and Allaite's face, but Zalaigh didn't seem shocked.

"How did you figure it out?" Zalaigh brushed his hand over the medallion resting on his chest.

"Yesterday you were weak and shaky. Today, you're hale and healthy. I don't really think good sex and a lot of rest would make that big of a change in you." Vlatko shot Rue a wink.

Rue laughed and Zalaigh might have blushed. It was hard to tell with the Mitcovian's skin colour.

"You have discovered the truth about our protection here on Mitcov. When I became the high councillor, my life force merged with the Heart. As long as I'm touching or in the vicinity of the stone, I'm fine. The longer I'm away from it, the weaker I become."

Rue looked sick. "Shit. You would have died if I had sold the gem."

"Yes. Why does that bother you?" Zalaigh nodded his thanks as Allaite poured him a glass of juice.

Rue's cheeks flushed and Vlatko had the oddest thought his lover was embarrassed.

"I might be a thief, but I've never killed anyone, or stolen from a mark that couldn't afford to lose what I took."

Allaite snorted and Vlatko frowned. As far-fetched as it might sound, he believed Rue.

"I know what it's like to have nothing. I'm not going to destroy someone for my gain." Rue shrugged, fluttering his hands over his plate. "I know you think I knew what gem I was stealing. I didn't even know the IUM had hired me. I was contacted by a middle-man and he gave me the specifics of the job."

Vlatko could tell the Mitcovians were sceptical. He didn't want to discuss that particular subject anymore. "Does the IUM know your life is tied to the stone?"

Zalaigh shook his head. "I don't believe so. It's only the high councillor and the head of security that are told the truth."

"If you were to die, would that affect the Heart and the net around the planet?" Vlatko asked, ignoring the sudden tension flowing from Allaite.

"No. The Heart would immediately attach itself to another person. In many ways, the Heart has a mind of its own. It chooses who the next high councillor will be. Do you really think I sought this position?"

Zalaigh pushed his plate away from him. He leaned his elbows on the table, studying the marble top. "I was a nondescript scientist. I didn't have any ambition to be anything other than that. I didn't even have any urge to be rich. I wanted to live an uneventful life with Allaite. One day, the former high councillor was visiting my laboratory and the Heart flared the instant he stepped into the room. Next thing I know, he's handing me the medallion and thanking the gods."

"That probably should have been our first clue that being high councillor wasn't the picnic they make it out to be." Allaite sighed.

"It flared when Rue touched it yesterday." Vlatko was afraid of what that might mean.

"Don't worry. Rue has power, but only a Mitcovian can be high councillor." Zalaigh glanced at the clock standing in the corner. "Come. We'll go to my lab. I'd like to do some blood work on you, Vlatko, to see what kind of damage the body armour is inflicting. Plus we'll discuss your symptoms."

"We may have forced your hand, Zalaigh, but I do thank you for trying this." Vlatko placed his hand on the small of Rue's back, allowing the Mitcovians to lead the way.

* * * *

Uncertain about what he should be doing, Rue stood in the corner of the room, watching as Zalaigh drew two vials of blood from Vlatko. He stayed out of the way and tried not to interrupt their conversation. Allaite leaned against the wall next to him.

"He loves this shit, doesn't he?" Rue gestured to where Zalaigh stooped over a microscope, checking some of Vlatko's blood.

"It was one of his attributes that first attracted me." Allaite winked at him. "Then I found out there were other parts of him I really enjoyed."

He couldn't stop from laughing aloud. Zalaigh glared at them. Vlatko smiled.

"Oops. Now we've irritated him," Allaite said under his breath to Rue. "Hey, Vlatko, I'm going to take your pretty boy here on a tour of the compound."

Rue started to protest the 'pretty boy' comment, but Vlatko nodded. "Take him, but you're responsible for him. He better come back in the same condition he left here."

"Hey, I can take care of myself," he grumbled.

"Don't worry. He won't even stub his toe. I'll keep a close eye on his fine ass."

"Not that close of an eye, I'm sure." Vlatko raised an eyebrow in Allaite's direction. "He's marked property." The assassin pointed to the bite mark on Rue's neck.

"Hello, I'm in the same fucking room as you." Rue crossed his arms and pouted.

Zalaigh rested against the counter and laughed. "My darling thief, I don't think they're really interested in where you are at the moment. Two big tough guys like our lovers have to push and shove to see who the alpha dog is."

"I'm not taking part in any pissing contest." Rue stomped towards the door, forgetting he needed to pass by Vlatko on his way out.

Vlatko snagged his arm and pulled him between those thick thighs. Vlatko cupped his chin with his rough hand, holding his fact still as Vlatko kissed him hard. Vlatko didn't ask for entrance, he demanded it. Rue opened for him, knowing he'd never really deny the man anything, especially when it came to enjoying

Vlatko's body. He wound his arms around the man's waist, pressing as close as he could get. Vlatko cradled his ass and squeezed hard, swallowing his moan.

He lost track of time as Vlatko devoured his mouth, nibbling and sucking. He was teetering on the edge of a climax when he heard clapping. He jerked away from Vlatko, remembering the Mitcovians were still in the room. Zalaigh grinned and gave him a slight nod. Allaite clapped again.

"Bravo. Expert display of ownership." The security officer praised Vlatko.

Rue studied Vlatko closely. The assassin stared back without blinking. In those dark eyes, he saw the truth. Vlatko hadn't kissed him to prove his ownership of Rue. He'd kissed him because he wanted nothing more than to taste Rue. Vlatko had forgotten about the other men in the room as much as Rue had.

"Get the hell out of here. There's no point in you hanging around being bored." Vlatko slapped his ass, ignoring Allaite's comments.

"He's right," Zalaigh agreed. The Mitcovian gestured to the vials. "We'll be doing tests and evaluating him for a while. I'll make sure Allaite brings you back here when we're through."

Rue took one more look at Vlatko and nodded. He turned to the enormous security officer. "Lead me astray, Allaite."

"With pleasure, Mr Thaday." Allaite opened the door, bowing as Rue walked by.

"Don't worry. Allaite will keep Rue safe," Zalaigh reassured Vlatko as he watched their lovers leave the lab.

Vlatko grunted. "I know."

"Allaite might be upset about the way Rue acquired the Heart, but he respects the thief for coming here and bargaining to save the life of someone he loves. It's something Allaite might do." Zalaigh pointed to Vlatko's shirt. "That has to come off."

Vlatko pulled it off, forgetting about the burn mark until Zalaigh's sharp intake of breath. He checked his shoulder in the mirror on the wall across from him. He was right—it had scarred. He had a red burn in the shape of a bird's claw.

"Knew she was going to mark me," he muttered.

"Where'd you get that?" Zalaigh's eyes gleamed.

"A firebird gave it to me a couple of days before we left the planet I'd been living on." He jumped when Zalaigh grabbed his arm.

"Did she speak to you?"

He nodded, wary of the excitement in the high councillor's voice.

"What did she say?"

Vlatko frowned, trying to remember everything the firebird had said. "Just something about coming to the planet long ago. She said Rue was more than a thief, but he didn't need to know about his past." He shot Zalaigh a sharp glance. "Do you know what she is?"

"I've only seen one of her kind when I was young. The firebird is so beautiful."

Vlatko was intrigued by the awed expression on Zalaigh's face. "Are there more of them around? Where do they come from?"

Zalaigh focused on him. "First, we'll take care of you and then I'll discuss the firebird with you and Rue. He is the most important part of this story."

Vlatko didn't like that answer, but figured there was no way he'd get Zalaigh to tell him anything else. "Let's get this done."

"Don't like being away from him, huh?" Zalaigh chuckled. "Ah, new love. I vaguely remember what that was like."

"Like you and Allaite don't spend every waking moment together."

"True." Zalaigh began to examine Vlatko's chest muscles. "Tell me, what made you throw everything away?"

"Which time?"

"You do seem to be an 'all or nothing' guy. This time, by coming here with Thaday? You threw away all that research." Zalaigh pressed on the spot where Vlatko's arm met his shoulder.

Pain shot through him and he barely suppressed the urge to knock the Mitcovian on his ass.

"I didn't throw my research away. I brought it with me if you'd like to look at it. Don't think there's much there that'll help you. I wasn't created to be smart." He clenched his teeth as Zalaigh's fingers kept investigating and the pain got worse.

"I'd like to see it. Even though you weren't trained for it, you might have gotten lucky. Desperate men like you make some amazing discoveries. This spot." Zalaigh pushed on Vlatko's back just below his right shoulder blade.

"Fuck," Vlatko yelled. He tried to pull away, but Zalaigh wouldn't let him.

"That's the point of origin. More than likely the IUM injected the liquid into your body right here. It's destabilising the fastest because it's had the highest exposure to the chemicals."

He felt Zalaigh's fingers trail over his spine down towards his ass. "Is there something wrong with my ass?" He didn't like anyone touching him except Rue.

"Hmm…" Zalaigh's touch disappeared from his skin. "Sorry. I was thinking."

"Just watch where those hands go. I don't think Allaite—or Rue, for that matter—would be happy about you feeling me up." He smiled at the horrified look on the Mitcovian's face. "I'm not that repulsive, am I?"

"Oh no! I'm sorry. I tend to touch things when I'm thinking." Zalaigh winked. "Actually, you are totally my type. If I didn't think our lovers would kill us, I'd be interested, but I don't think I'm your type."

"I never thought I had a type until I met Rue. It was whoever was handy at the time, but when I saw him, I realised whoever was handy always looked an awful lot like Rue." He shrugged.

"Why travel with him to trade the stone? Were you afraid he'd change his mind and disappear with it?" Zalaigh picked up his shirt and set it next to him.

"I won't say the thought hadn't crossed my mind, but I'd decided it didn't matter. Either way I was dead. I could stay on that planet and die alone or I could go wherever Rue was going and enjoy myself for once in my life." He paused, wondering if he should say anything about Rue's touch. A glance at Zalaigh made Vlatko figure he probably already knew about it.

"Plus there's something in Rue's hands. When he touches me, I feel as if I'm bathed in heat. The pain can get to the point where I'd cut my arm off rather than live with it one second more. He takes it away."

Zalaigh's expression was thoughtful. "When he touches you?"

"Yeah."

"I'll have to think about that. I want to run some tests. Lie down on the table." Zalaigh wheeled over a cart.

Vlatko lifted his legs on to the table and lay back, ignoring the pain. He'd think about how Rue looked when they fucked. It'd take his mind off the uncomfortable tests Zalaigh was going to do.

* * * *

Rue shut his mouth with a snap. His hands itched. Allaite was showing him around Zalaigh's house. He'd never seen so many baubles just begging him to pick them up and pocket them. He stuck his hands behind his back, entwining his fingers to keep from touching things.

The room teemed with treasures from throughout the universe. Venuvian crystals sat next to dark Ecofo amber. Diamonds, gold and rare paintings graced the walls. He walked from one piece to another, trying to guess how much he'd get for them on the open market. Allaite rested a hip against one of the Milatout antique chests and watched him.

"Why would you bring me here?" Rue turned to study the Mitcovian. "I never said I stopped stealing."

"That's true, but I figure you know what side of the toast is buttered. You're not going to do anything to upset us until after Vlatko's healed."

Rue ignored the unspoken *if he can be* that lingered at the end of Allaite's sentence. He was doing his best not to think about Vlatko not making it. "You're right. You're the only thing standing between me and an IUM firing squad."

Allaite shrugged. "We can afford to be generous now that the IUM isn't hanging over us."

"Officer Allaite, I've been waiting for hours to talk to the high councillor. I demand to know why I've been denied an audience with him."

Rue and Allaite turned to see the guard at the door restraining a short, dumpy man. The stranger was dressed in a black and silver uniform with the emblem of the IUM embroidered on the chest. Rue managed to move away from Allaite, not wanting the emissary to notice him.

Allaite grabbed Rue's hand and shook his head. "The high councillor is attending to some important business, sir. I'm sure as soon as he is done, he'll be happy to talk to you."

"I've heard that same bullshit for two weeks now. It isn't good to keep the IUM waiting. Our patience wears thin." The envoy's words were an ill-concealed threat.

"You voice threats in the high councillor's house, Marca. How dare you?" Allaite bared his teeth in a snarl. "I'll inform him of your warning. He'll grant you an audience when he is ready. Not a minute sooner."

Marca flinched at the anger in Allaite's voice and Rue felt a shiver of fear race down his own spine. He never wanted the security officer mad at him.

"Escort Envoy Marca to his suite. I'm sure he'll enjoy dining there tonight." Allaite turned his back on the IUM officer. "Did you get a chance to see the fire opal? It was brought to Mitcov thousands of years ago by Earth men looking for a new home."

Rue could feel the envoy's glare burning a hole in his back. He hoped the man didn't know who he was or everything would be screwed. "Do you think he knows who I am?" he whispered under his breath to Allaite.

The Mitcovian shrugged. "Doesn't matter now. Even if Zalaigh hadn't pledged protection to you and Vlatko, something tells me the Councillor's Heart wouldn't allow anything to happen to you." Allaite gestured to where a large fire opal sat on a glass pedestal.

Rue stopped and stared at the gem. It was the size of his fist. "It shines so brightly."

"Yes and since it was brought here, it has remained untouched, except for a small piece that was chipped off to create the Heart. Unfortunately, the spell or power used to make the Heart has been lost through the centuries, so we can't make another one." Allaite checked his watch. "We'll go back. Zalaigh should be done running his tests."

"Hopefully he'll have figured out a treatment for Vlatko." Rue was eager to get back to his lover.

"Don't hope for miracles, thief. Zalaigh is a talented scientist, but some solutions are beyond even his brilliant mind."

Rue studied his feet for a second. "I know and I'm trying not to get my hopes up because I've always been disappointed in the past. I've just got a hunch that we'll figure out a cure here."

"We'll help all we can." Allaite led the way back to Zalaigh's lab.

Rue knew the Mitcovians would do all they could to save Vlatko, but a little voice in his head wasn't sure what they could do.

Chapter Thirteen

Vlatko looked up as the door to the lab opened. Rue entered, followed by Allaite. Vlatko gave the thief a small smile. Rue strolled over to him and rested his hand on Vlatko's back. He couldn't keep back a sigh as the heat from Rue's hand seeped into his muscles.

"Does it hurt there?" Rue traced circles on Vlatko's skin.

"Try an inch or two higher and to your right," Zalaigh suggested.

Rue followed the high councillor's directions and Vlatko almost leapt from the table. He clenched his teeth to keep from crying out. Even with the warmth coming from Rue, the pain was excruciating.

"Keep your palm pressed against the spot. He's been in pain for a while. I'm hoping you can help alleviate some of it." Zalaigh turned back to the test results.

Vlatko closed his eyes, absorbing and enjoying the relief Rue gave him. "Did you have a nice tour?"

"I took him to the treasure vault." Allaite's voice came from the far end of the room.

"Were you trying to torture him with things he couldn't steal?" Vlatko joked, then grunted as his ass received a hard pinch.

"I'll have you know, if I was so inclined, I could steal everything in that room. I have some ethics, though, and it wouldn't be right to steal from the Mitcovians while they're trying to help us." Rue sounded indignant.

Vlatko rolled to his side and wrapped an arm around Rue's waist. He grinned up at the thief. "I'm glad ethics didn't stop you from letting me fuck you while you were trying to steal from me."

"I know a good thing when I see it. I wasn't about to let you go without giving you a try." Rue cupped Vlatko's cock and stroked him through his pants.

"Don't start something we can't finish, love. There are other people in the room." He rubbed his own hands over Rue's ass.

"Don't let that stop you," Allaite encouraged them. "Gods, you two are like horny teenagers."

Vlatko stuck his tongue out at the security officer. "You're just jealous."

"Maybe." Allaite admitted, earning a swat from Zalaigh.

They laughed. Allaite touched the high councillor's hand. "We have to do something about the envoy from the IUM. He confronted us in the treasure vault."

Zalaigh frowned. Vlatko sat up, grabbing Rue by the arms. "He didn't see you, did he?"

Rue shook his head. "I don't think so."

"It doesn't matter if he did. Any plans they made are finished and the IUM can't do a thing about it." Allaite stated calmly.

"They don't know that. If they know who Rue is, they'll think he's here to double-cross them." Panic rose in Vlatko's heart.

"Take a deep breath, Vlatko. I *am* here to double-cross them." Rue held his face in his slender hands. "We're safe."

"Still, until the envoy leaves, you're not allowed to go anywhere alone. They aren't going to accept you returning the Heart without a fight. They might not be able to get to the stone, but they can kill you to get revenge." He gazed into the amber eyes he'd grown to love.

"What's to be gained by killing him?" Zalaigh asked. "He's a thief and he's already given away what they want."

"To set an example for anyone else who might think about screwing the IUM. By killing Rue, it's as if they're saying 'See what happens to double-crossing thieves.'" Vlatko hoped he was getting his fears across.

Allaite narrowed his eyes in thought then nodded. "There'll be a guard available for those times when you can't be with him."

Rue protested. "I'm capable of taking care of myself."

"I know, and usually I wouldn't do this, but the IUM might send an assassin. You're not equipped to deal with that." Vlatko rubbed his hands together.

It was the truth. Against any other type of attack, Vlatko believed Rue could handle it, but the assassins were a whole different set of bad guys. Rue's mind was devious and always looking for the advantage. He wasn't a killer.

"I thought you said they weren't creating more assassins." Rue sat next to him, resting a hand on his leg.

"Their scientists can't make any more like me. I stole the formula for the armour and the genetic code needed for the accelerated healing. They can no longer breed children with superior strength or speed. There are maybe fifty to a hundred assassins like me. Our ranks are getting smaller as we die. The IUM is back to square one with their assassin programme." Vlatko leaned against Rue.

"You have all that information?" Zalaigh enquired, looking thoughtful.

Vlatko nodded.

"Where? I'd love to do some research on those formulas." Excitement played in Zalaigh's voice.

Vlatko tapped the back of his head. "It's all right here."

"You've memorised them?" Zalaigh sounded shocked. "We'll have to get you to write them down."

He shook his head. "No, I mean they're on a small chip I had placed under the skin at the base of my skull."

Zalaigh grabbed an electronic wand off the counter and passed the end of it over Vlatko. It beeped and a red image about four inches wide showed up. "Damn. That had to hurt."

"Yeah. Had a huge headache for a while afterwards, but made it easier to carry. No paper trail."

Rue chuckled. "He let me search his chambers looking for stuff I'd never find."

"Bit of an asshole, huh?" Allaite slapped Vlatko's back.

Vlatko grimaced at the pain sliding down his spine, but he nodded. "Couldn't think of any other reason to get him to stick around."

Rue snuggled close to him and he soaked up the thief's body heat.

"Will you let me retrieve the chip?" Zalaigh pulled out a small tray with surgical instruments on it.

Rue started to protest, but Vlatko stopped him. "It needs to come out and I'll be fine in a day or two."

Vlatko lay down. Zalaigh pushed his braids out of the way. The high councillor found the bare spot left after the implant was put in.

"At least we won't have to cut your hair. I'll give you a shot to deaden the pain."

Vlatko heard Zalaigh shifting some things around beside him. "Don't worry about that. There won't be much and I can deal with it. The tissue has grown around it so it's going to be deeper than when it was originally put in."

"But..."

Vlatko knew not giving him anaesthesia went against everything Zalaigh had learnt. "I have a huge tolerance for pain, Zalaigh. You could probably perform most surgeries on me and I'd never feel anything. Just do it."

Rue managed to choke back the contents of his stomach when Zalaigh made the first incision. Blood welled up and Zalaigh swore.

"Allaite, grab some gauze and mop up the blood. I need to be able to see where the chip is."

Rue reached out to grip Vlatko's hand. Vlatko shifted slightly and Rue sat down in the chair Allaite pushed towards him. Vlatko's dark eyes met his and he had the nerve to smile.

"Not used to seeing brain surgery?"

Rue swallowed. "I'm not used to seeing any type of surgery. Especially when the person is awake."

"At one point, all patients were awake for any kind of surgery. That was before they figured out how to kill the pain without killing the patient. Even brain surgery was performed that way." Zalaigh's comment was distracted as he made the incision wider and deeper.

Closing his eyes, Rue took a deep breath. A pressure on his hand made him look, afraid to see Vlatko in some sort of pain. His lover gave him a wink.

"It'll be okay," Vlatko whispered, eyes crossing at a particularly deep poke from Zalaigh. "If you need to, just look away. Don't focus on the blood."

"You need to stop talking before I hit something more vital than tissue." Zalaigh's voice was fierce as he concentrated on finding the chip.

"He'll be quiet." Rue gave Vlatko a glare.

Vlatko pouted but didn't say anything else. Rue kept a tight hold of Vlatko's hand, needing the contact for himself, even if Vlatko wasn't bothered by the surgery.

Ten minutes later, with bloody gauze littering the floor and Rue positive he was going to pass out, Zalaigh gave a triumphant cry. He looked up to see the high councillor holding a small black object in his forceps.

"Allaite, grab a bowl and bring it over here."

Rue flinched as the chip hit the steel bowl with a ping.

"We'll sew you up and you can rest for a while."

Rue managed to watch as Zalaigh stitched up the incision. He winced each time the needle pierced Vlatko's flesh, but Vlatko didn't seem to notice.

"All done. Be careful when you sit up." Zalaigh patted Vlatko's shoulder and gave Rue a reassuring smile.

Vlatko didn't move. Hysteria began to well in Rue's mind. "Is he dead?" He wanted to scream the words, but they came out as a harsh whisper.

Allaite leaned over Vlatko for a moment then laughed. "He's not dead. He's asleep."

Rue prised open his hand and let Vlatko's drop to the table. The jolt didn't wake the assassin. Rue reached out, shaking Vlatko. "Wake up, asshole. You're not supposed to fall asleep during surgery."

Vlatko's eyes slowly opened and dark eyes blinked at him, bleary and confused. "What's wrong?"

"You went to sleep while some guy was poking sharp objects into your flesh," Rue pointed out, proud of himself for not yelling at Vlatko.

Vlatko sat up. Allaite and Zalaigh were poised to catch him if he needed support. Rue watched Vlatko scrub his hands over his face and reach behind to probe the spot where the implant had been.

Rue batted Vlatko's fingers away. "You're not supposed to touch it."

"Sorry." Vlatko set his feet on the floor and stood up. There was no hesitation. No struggling to find his balance. Vlatko grimaced and stretched tired muscles. "So I fell asleep."

"Yes. Normal people don't do that. I thought you didn't need sleep." Rue stroked his hand over Vlatko's bare arm.

"Normally I don't, but it's been a stressful day. My body must have decided it needed to take some time out." Vlatko encircled his waist with a strong arm. "Let's go back to our room. I think we both need a nap."

Rue rested his head on Vlatko's chest and sighed. "You're right. This whole experience has been a little overwhelming, even for me."

"I'll have dinner sent to your suite. Clean the sutures, and in a week I'll take them out." Zalaigh leaned against Allaite, watching them with sympathetic eyes.

"Thanks, but don't worry. They'll be ready to come out tomorrow."

Rue let Vlatko guide him to the door. Exhaustion swamped him. His hand ached from holding onto Vlatko so tightly. He stumbled and Vlatko stopped, sweeping him into his arms.

"Put me down, idiot. You just had your flesh cut open and something removed." Rue punched at Vlatko's arms.

"You don't weigh that much, love. I'll be fine carrying you."

Vlatko didn't stop and Rue didn't have the energy to argue with him anymore. He laid his head back down, letting Vlatko do his caveman routine. He couldn't help the secret thrill it gave him, having Vlatko carry him.

* * * *

Zalaigh watched Vlatko and Rue disappear around the corner. He sighed, rubbing a hand over his head. He was tired and it wasn't even dinner time yet—he'd done more stuff so far today than his normal day called for. It felt good to be doing something useful again.

"You missed it, didn't you?" Allaite gripped his shoulders, squeezing and working on his tense muscles.

"Missed what?" Zalaigh shuffled the papers around, trying to find a pattern or something to give him a clue as to what would work for Vlatko.

"The research. The numbers. All the confusion and headache involved with solving a science problem that might save a man's life." Allaite nuzzled the side of Zalaigh's face.

He laughed. "If you'd said something like that a week ago, I'd have told you no. I didn't miss it at all. Too much stress and too much riding on me finding a solution. Now that I've started this, I want to find the key to fixing the problem I helped create in the first place."

Allaite slipped his hands down and wrapped his arms around his chest, pulling him back against his muscled body. "It's not your fault. You knew the formula was flawed. It's the IUM's fault for using it without testing it. Vlatko isn't blaming you either, so don't accept guilt that isn't yours."

Zalaigh rested his head on Allaite's shoulder. "Yes, love. You do realise that before I became high councillor, I never really let guilt eat me alive or make me feel bad. Maybe there's something about being connected to the Heart, ensuring my need to keep people safe and healthy." He closed his eyes, but saw the lines of numbers scrolling across the insides of his eyelids. "There's something about Vlatko's blood niggling at my mind, but I can't put my finger on it."

"Maybe you should go and take a nap as well," Allaite suggested while running warm palms over Zalaigh's tunic. "You're still recovering from having the Heart returned. I'm sure it'll all be clearer when you're rested."

"You're right. We'll have dinner in our suite. Also, send a note to the IUM envoy. I'll meet with him tomorrow. Make sure Rue and Vlatko are there as well." Zalaigh gathered the papers up, stuffing them into a file.

"Are you sure Vlatko will be up to confronting Marca?" Allaite held open the door for him.

"He said he would be fine tomorrow and I believe him. The accelerated healing process the IUM managed to create in him seems to be rather remarkable." Zalaigh moved down the hallway. "I'll download all of the information off the chip tomorrow afternoon and we'll see what I can do with all those formulas."

"Okay. I'll let the guys know and I'll arrange for extra guards in the conference room. I don't trust the IUM any further than I can throw that *baisha*." Allaite kept one hand on Zalaigh's arm.

Zalaigh knew his lover was on guard against any attacks. Now that Rue had returned the Heart, the situation had changed and they could throw the envoy off the planet. But until they got the IUM off Mitcov, Allaite wouldn't lower his vigilance and Zalaigh was happy about that.

"Do you have time to nap with me?" He ran his hand over Allaite's sapphire skin.

"Yes. My lieutenant knows where to find me if there's trouble, but I think everything will be quiet tonight."

Zalaigh hoped so. He slept better with Allaite next to him and he really did need more rest. "Great."

He waited until Allaite pushed open the door to their suite and checked all the rooms before he moved from just inside the entrance. Allaite had lectured him until the poor Mitcovian was hoarse about taking precautions for his safety. His lover gestured for him to join him in the bathing room. He tossed the files on the couch as he walked past. He'd go over them later that night.

* * * *

Vlatko bit back a groan as he rolled onto his back. Rue shifted, crawling over to cover him like a blanket. He cupped Rue's ass and stroked those firm muscles with his thumbs. His head throbbed and Vlatko knew he'd never get back to sleep. He slowly moved Rue back to the mattress. Rue's eyes opened slightly.

"What's wrong?" Rue murmured.

"Can't sleep. I'm going for a walk." Vlatko tucked the covers around Rue and kissed the thief's forehead.

"You want me to go with you?"

Vlatko smiled. "No. Just go back to sleep."

"Be careful." Rue turned and buried his face in Vlatko's pillow.

"I will," Vlatko promised as he let himself out of their suite.

A movement caught his gaze and he tensed. A Mitcovian guard stepped from an alcove. Vlatko headed towards the guard.

"I'm going to wander a bit. Can't sleep. Keep an eye on the door and make sure no one goes in, especially if you don't know him."

The Mitcovian saluted. "Yes, sir. There are guards around the perimeter of the house. No one will get in that way either."

"Good. I knew Allaite was thorough." Vlatko headed down the hall.

He didn't know where he was going. He just needed to move, to ease the ache in his head and body. Rue had given him a massage earlier when they'd got back to their rooms. Even the heat from his lover's hands hadn't been able to take all of the pain away. Vlatko had discovered sometimes there was nothing to do but walk, forcing the pain to work through his body. He flexed his hands. The weakness in them wasn't any worse than it had been on the other planet. Maybe the destruction had slowed.

He had learnt how to deal with the pain over the years as his body deteriorated. When he'd first started feeling it, he'd been shocked. After going most of his life without pain, to have it suddenly appear was almost too much. Sometimes he wondered if what he was feeling was all in his head. Vlatko knew he should hurt after having someone cut into his skull—maybe he was imagining the discomfort he felt? He shook his head and an ache welled in it. No, there definitely was something wrong. He'd walk to see if he could ease it.

Zalaigh's house gleamed silver in the moonlight. Vlatko wondered if he could find the kitchen. He'd been asleep when dinner was delivered and Rue hadn't wanted to wake him. He moved farther into the back part of the house, taking a set of back stairs down to the first floor. The house was quiet except for the occasional creak of wood or soft shut of doors as late-night travellers moved throughout the building.

Vlatko kept an eye out for anyone looking suspicious, but by the time he made it to the back of the first floor and actually found the kitchen, he hadn't seen anyone. He pulled open the refrigerator and searched the shelves. He yanked different packages out, setting them on the island counter. Vlatko rooted around the drawers. He placed a plate and a set of silverware next to the food. After fixing several sandwiches, he settled down to eat.

"Ah, you're losing your touch, friend. I could have killed you before you realised I was there."

After whirling around, Vlatko sent a serrated knife flying through the air before embedding itself in the wall next to the man who had spoken. The man's eyes widened, but there was no fear in them.

"Maybe I was wrong." He went and sat across the island from Vlatko.

"I've known you were behind me since I hit the first floor. Who are you here to kill?" Vlatko pushed his second sandwich towards the man.

The man studied the food then looked up at Vlatko. Whatever was in Vlatko's gaze must have satisfied him, because he picked it up and started eating. "I came to kill the high councillor when the time was right, but now I'm thinking there won't be a right time. What are you here for? I thought you'd quit working for the IUM?"

Vlatko grabbed the jug of Mitcovian ale and poured himself a drink. "I'm not here for the IUM, I'm here to see if I can find a cure for our particular ailment."

The other assassin stared at him. "Why here? Do you really think you'll learn something?"

"The scientist who first invented the body armour was a Mitcovian. The IUM stole his formulas and research from him before he had a chance to stabilise the chemicals. I'm dead anyway, Three. Coming here can't hurt me." Vlatko swirled the ale around in his glass.

"Is the scientist even alive still?" There was a faint hint of hope in Three's voice.

"Yeah. He's helping me and that's why I need you not to kill the high councillor." Vlatko figured nothing was gained by not telling the other assassin who the scientist really was. "Before he became high councillor, Zalaigh was the scientist working on the formula."

"No fucking way!" Three jumped to his feet and started to pace. "I came within days of killing the one person who might be able to save my worthless ass."

"Three, there's more. You'll want to be off planet by sunrise," Vlatko informed his associate. "The Heart has been returned. There's no way the IUM will be taking over Mitcov."

"Shit. This night keeps getting better and better. How the hell did they get that stone back? The little asshole hired to steal it is either still in hiding or he's already sold it on the open market." Three threw his arms up in the air.

"Actually, that little asshole is sleeping in my bed at the moment. He decided to return the Heart to the Mitcovians for their help in finding a cure for me." Vlatko hid his smile behind his hand at the thought of Rue's naked body in bed.

"Really? Well, you'd better be prepared to protect him because, as soon as the commanders find out he double-crossed them, they'll send out a hit on him." Three threw a glance over at Vlatko.

"I realise that, but they'll have to come through the entire Mitcovian army, their security officers and me. Plus I think the Heart likes him, so it might protect him as well."

"You always did enjoy throwing monkey wrenches into perfectly good plans." Three shook his head. "A cure, huh? Would you contact me if you ever do find one? I'll take myself out of the chain of command and let them send someone else after your boyfriend."

"Sure. I'll have Stargazer get in touch with you the moment I learn anything." Vlatko held out a hand to the assassin. "I know you'll keep your word."

"Stargazer? The little weasel still owes me money," Three grumbled, but shook Vlatko's hand. "Take care of yourself, man, and watch your back."

"I will." Vlatko watched Three fade into the shadows. He had no doubts his fellow assassin would leave the planet. The older the assassin, the more likely it was they would be willing to leave things the way they were as long as their own lives might be spared.

"Whom were you talking to?" Allaite wandered in, wearing a simple white loincloth and nothing else.

Vlatko took out another glass and poured more ale for the security officer. "One of the IUM assassins. Three has been hanging around for a couple of days trying to get a chance at killing Zalaigh."

Allaite growled.

"Don't worry. He's leaving. He'll be off planet before the sun rises. He knows it's pointless to try since the Heart is back and he doesn't want to kill the man who might know how to stop our deaths."

"Looking out for himself, huh?" Allaite gulped down the ale, gesturing for Vlatko to fill it up again.

"We aren't concerned with other people. How can we be if our primary purpose is to kill them?" Vlatko shrugged. "You appeal to what matters most to them and that's their lives. He's gone and that's what's important."

"But there will be others?" Allaite jumped up and sat on the island next to Vlatko.

"Of course there will. The IUM isn't going to give up just because their first assassin failed at his job. They'll send more until you can convince them coming after Zalaigh will exact a higher price than even they want to pay." Vlatko leant back and stared up at Allaite.

"What about you?" Allaite gestured vaguely in the general direction of Vlatko's rooms. "They'll come after your lover as well."

"I'll protect Rue until my dying breath, whether I breathe it at the end of this month or twenty years from now. If I do go early, I expect you to keep him safe for me. Not only because your high councillor commanded, but because I've asked you." Vlatko held out his hand to the security officer. He knew Allaite was the second most powerful male on Mitcov and almost anything he promised would be held as law as well.

Allaite studied Vlatko for a second. He hid nothing from him. What was the point? Vlatko didn't know if Zalaigh could figure out a way to save him, so he had nothing to lose anymore when it came to his pride.

The Mitcovian nodded and grasped Vlatko's hand. "I expect you to do the same for me, if for some reason one of the IUM's assassins get me."

"Done. Our men will be protected." He took a bite of his sandwich. "What are you doing up?"

"Couldn't sleep. Too much to think about, with the meeting tomorrow with the emissary." Allaite jumped off the counter and grinned down at Vlatko. "Since you can't sleep either, what about a little workout?"

"I won't be at my best." Vlatko set his dishes in the sink then put the ale away.

"As far as I'm concerned, this is the perfect time to test you. If you were the best assassin they had, then I could learn things from you that would protect Zalaigh."

"True." Vlatko followed the large male out of the kitchen and into the Mitcovian night.

* * * *

Rue woke up as a warm body slid into bed next to him. He sighed as a heavy arm encircled his waist and snuggled him up against a solid chest. He stroked over the scarred hand resting on his stomach.

"Are you feeling better?"

Vlatko grunted. "A little. I worked out with Allaite. Gave him a few tips to help him protect Zalaigh."

"You really believe the IUM will send someone to kill Zalaigh, even after they find out the Heart is back?" He felt Vlatko's head move as the man nodded.

"Of course. The best way to protect you both is to expect an attack. The military will resent being shown up by you, a petty thief. So they will always be after you. That's why you might want to consider never leaving this planet or, if you do, take a security team with you." Vlatko's warm breath brushed over the nape of Rue's neck.

"Why will I need a team when I have you?" He entwined their fingers together, not wanting to lose touch with any part of this man's body.

"If Zalaigh finds a cure—"

"When he finds a cure," Rue interrupted. He wasn't willing to even think of failure.

"When he finds a cure." Vlatko's voice held a smile. "There's no guarantee any of my enhancements will survive whatever his cure is."

Rue thought about that. Would it be terrible if Vlatko lost all the advantages his superior genetics gave him? It would be—Vlatko had been raised for one purpose and that was to kill. When the body armour was stabilised or removed, what would Vlatko be trained to do? Rue made a mental note to talk to Allaite about using Vlatko as a guard. The assassin's specialised skills would make him perfect for protection details.

"We'll find something for you to do and I trust you'll take care of me." He pushed back closer to Vlatko, rubbing his ass against Vlatko's erection. "You could just stay with me and be my sex slave."

Vlatko laughed, sliding his hand down to cup Rue's cock and squeezing. "I could see the possibilities in that, but shouldn't a sex slave be willing to be fucked by his master?"

Rue shook his head. "Not my slave. He only has to be willing to fuck me whenever I want it."

He ran his hand over Vlatko's chest and up onto the shoulder where the scar was. He traced it, a puzzled frown forming as heat tingled along the tips of his fingers. Vlatko sucked in a breath, letting Rue know he felt the warmth as well.

"I wonder why she marked you like this," he murmured.

Vlatko shrugged. "I guess she didn't feel it was important for you to know."

"Somehow I get the feeling it is important. She just didn't want to tell us. She wanted to be a damned oracle." He felt a surge of anger rise in him.

"Hush. The firebird isn't like us. She's more of an alien to her world than we are to the Mitcovians. We must give her a little leeway." Vlatko brushed a hand over Rue's ass. "Now try to go back to sleep. It's going to be a long day tomorrow."

Rue decided arguing with Vlatko wasn't worth wasting energy over. He too had a feeling tomorrow was going to be rough.

Chapter Fourteen

Vlatko kept his gaze fixed on the door through which the IUM emissary would be entering. Allaite had ordered his men to search the emissary and any people he might bring with him, but Vlatko knew all the weapons that could be smuggled in under even the most vigilant eye. Rue stood next to the high councillor and Vlatko saw Zalaigh glance down at his lover with an aggravated frown.

He wondered what Rue was doing. Shifting a step closer, he saw Rue's foot tapping wildly against the tiled floor. Vlatko hid a smile. It seemed odd Rue could be so patient when it came to setting up and executing a heist, but when it came to waiting for anything else, the thief was annoyingly impatient. Zalaigh caught his gaze and gave him a questioning look. He shrugged. Threatening punishment wouldn't work because Rue liked a little pain once in a while.

Zalaigh gave a long suffering sigh, took Rue's hand in his and started walking around the room, pointing at the portraits and statues decorating the room.

Allaite moved over to stand by Vlatko for a second, his own eyes tracking the couple around the room.

"Zalaigh is being very good to him," Vlatko commented.

Allaite nodded. "In many ways, your lover is still young compared to us. He's learnt patience for his job, just not for his life yet."

"If he chooses to stay here, he'll learn it. I think Rue needs to feel safe."

Rue shot a glance over his shoulder, searching Vlatko out. Vlatko nodded at him and gave him a smile. Rue turned back to comment on something Zalaigh had said.

"Wherever he is, he'll only feel safe if you're with him, I believe. You seem to have spoilt him a little," Allaite pointed out.

Vlatko feared that. In case Zalaigh couldn't find a cure, he didn't want Rue cast adrift, scared and stealing again. "That's why you have to take care of him if I'm not around."

Allaite squeezed Vlatko's shoulder. "I gave you my word and I'll honour that. Even if I don't find your young lover charming."

A knock sounded on the door and they moved back to their original positions. Vlatko clasped the grip of his 3.30 laser. The first threatening move towards either Zalaigh or Rue would bring death to whoever made it. His life and his love were represented in the two men in the middle of the room and he wouldn't lose either without a fight.

The IUM emissary stalked into the room, finger pointed at Zalaigh. "High Councillor, it's about time you deigned to see me. I don't appreciate being treated like a supplicant. The Inter-Universal Military is very powerful and you risk much, brushing them off for days."

Zalaigh moved and Allaite tensed. The high councillor held out his hand to the emissary. At that moment, a beam of sunlight came through the window and highlighted the red stone in the medallion Zalaigh was wearing. The emissary gasped, ignoring the hand, and reached for the medallion. Allaite shot forward, grabbing the man's wrist and jerking him away from Zalaigh.

"No one touches the Councillor's Heart," the Mitcovian security officer growled.

"Where did you get that?" Marca's eyes widened when he saw Rue standing behind Zalaigh. "I should have known you'd double-cross us. Thieves have no honour and we should never have trusted you."

"So you're admitting the IUM hired this man to steal the Heart and turn it over to you." Zalaigh glared at Marca.

The emissary didn't even have the decency to look ashamed. "Of course we did."

"You aren't even going to deny it?" Allaite spoke up.

Marca shook his head. "What's the point? Sure, I could throw a fit and say he's lying, and that you could trust us. But we both know differently. I'm not going to waste my time or yours." Marca turned to head out of the room. He stopped at the doorway, turning to give them all one last warning. "This isn't the end of it. The Heart returning is a minor setback. The IUM will have Mitcov. Watch your back, High Councillor. You too, Thaday. No one double-crosses us."

"You're threatening them in the high councillor's own house?" Vlatko shielded Rue.

"It's not a threat. It's a promise. So you brought him here," Marca sneered at Rue. "Did this killer convince you to forfeit your life so he could find a cure?" The envoy pointed to Vlatko. "There is no cure, and by taking our files you've condemned your own kind to a painful death as well."

"The IUM scientists haven't been able to find a solution to the problem. Your assassins are dying. The only way we have a choice about our death is if we allow someone to kill us." Vlatko stiffened, ready to jump on Marca, but Rue tugged on one of his braids and he relaxed.

The emissary was trying to get one of them to attack him, thus giving the IUM reason to declare Mitcov an outlaw planet, then move in to quell the rebellion.

"We won't play your game, Marca. Get out of here. Rellam, take the emissary to the transport pad. His belongings are already there." Zalaigh gestured to one of the guards. "I'll give you one warning. Any attempt to harm either of these men will result in an immediate retaliation from us against the perpetrator."

Marca acknowledged the high councillor's warning and left. The tension hanging thick in the room relaxed. Rue wiggled under Vlatko's arm and pressed against his side.

"We faced the bad guys down. We won," the thief crowed.

"Don't celebrate until the man's off this planet. We'll have to keep an eye out for several months. After a while, they'll turn their attention to some other planet easier to destroy." Vlatko tightened his grip on Rue. "We just have to wait them out."

"You're right." Zalaigh sighed and brushed his hands off on the long, flowing, midnight-blue tunic he wore. The Mitcovian turned to look at Vlatko. "I've run some more tests. I think I have an idea of how to cure you. Come with me."

Rue squeezed his waist in excitement, but Vlatko wasn't planning his future yet until he saw proof the cure was working. They followed Zalaigh to the lab.

Rue could tell Vlatko didn't want to get his hopes up, but Rue wasn't willing to entertain the idea of Vlatko not living forever. He didn't worry about anything happening to him. His thieving days were over, even if Vlatko died. Something had changed in him and it wasn't any fun anymore to plan and plot a heist. He laid his head on Vlatko's shoulder as they stopped to wait while Zalaigh opened the lab door.

"Part of the problem with the body armour molecules is that they begin to thicken over time. It's causing blockages in your veins and arteries. Those blockages weaken your muscles. Plus, it also acts as an accelerator. The natural decay of your cells is sped up by the body armour's own instability. I think we need to do some radiation treatments." Zalaigh pointed to a chair. "Sit there."

"Radiation? What's that?" Rue knew about the radiation one could get from being exposed to too much sunlight. He'd never thought it would be a good health cure.

"In the old days of Earth, they used to use radiation and chemotherapy to cure cancer." Zalaigh caught Rue's puzzled frown. "Cancer isn't a disease we see anymore. Around the twenty-third Earth century, they managed to find a way to prevent it. I've read journals about the treatments. They tended to make people sick and very tired for around three days after each treatment. I'm not sure what it'll do to you, since your healing powers are far superior to a normal human's."

Vlatko stripped off his shirt, handing it to Rue. Rue lifted it to his face and breathed deep. His lover's scent filled his nose. His cock got hard and he wanted to beg Vlatko to bend him over the examining table. Fucking him until he screamed sounded better than taking some medicine that was going to make Vlatko sick. Rue winced as Zalaigh pierced Vlatko's skin right above the man's heart with the thin laser scalpel.

"What's that for? Won't the body armour stop that?" Rue felt his own skin crawl as Zalaigh fed the slender line into Vlatko's vein.

"No. This goes into the vein. The chemo and radiation will go in there. Hopefully it'll help. We'll give you several treatments and then, after a month or two, we'll see what happens." Zalaigh hooked a bag onto a stand then attached the end of the plastic tubing to the other sticking out of Vlatko's chest.

Rue swallowed and a wave of dizziness caused him to sway. Vlatko reached for him, but Zalaigh stopped him.

"Don't move. I don't want you to tear the line out." Zalaigh pushed Rue into a chair next to Vlatko. "Sit down before you fall over. I don't want to have to fix you up. My stitching skills aren't that good."

"Maybe you should go find something else to do, Rue. You don't seem to enjoy these trips to Zalaigh's lab and I don't want you to have to sit here while I'm getting treated." Vlatko touched his leg with his other hand. "I'm sure Allaite or Zalaigh can find something for you to do."

Rue pouted. "You don't want me around."

He saw Vlatko's eyebrows rise until Rue smiled, and a matching one appeared on Vlatko's face. "You know

I'd love to have you around, but not if it makes you sick."

Allaite stuck his head around the door frame. "Are things going all right in here?"

"Yes, love. Though I was wondering if you could find something useful for Rue to do?" At Rue's protest, the high councillor shook his head. "If Vlatko wasn't starting his treatments, I would have found something for both of you to do. You're not going to be allowed to laze around here. I run a tight ship." The Mitcovian winked at him.

Rue sighed. He leaned over and brushed a kiss over Vlatko's cheek. "I'll stop by in an hour to see how you're doing."

"Don't worry, Rue. I'll be fine." Vlatko nodded at Allaite. "Go have fun and find something legal to do."

Chapter Fifteen

Two months later

Rue woke in the early morning hours. The Mitcovian sun wouldn't be up for a while, yet their moon cast enough light for him to see Vlatko clearly. The past two months had been hard on his lover. Vlatko was pale, or as pale as someone with dark mahogany skin could be. The treatments Zalaigh had devised wore the big man out.

No matter how stoic and uncomplaining Vlatko had been, Rue knew the treatments weren't working. The destruction of Vlatko's body progressed and Rue found himself faced with the very real possibility that Vlatko would die. The sadness welling in him made him restless. He climbed from the bed.

Vlatko shifted and mumbled. Rue stroked his hand over Vlatko's braids. A surge of thankfulness rose through him—Zalaigh had managed to make sure Vlatko wouldn't lose his hair. He kept petting Vlatko until the man settled back into a deep sleep. Rue didn't want to risk waking him up again, so he slid from the bedroom and made his way to the treasure room.

The guard stationed at the door of the vault nodded, opening the safe without comment. Allaite had told Rue he was welcome to visit the treasures whenever he wanted. Moving slowly from exquisite piece to piece, he found his worries dissolving. In some strange way, being surrounded by the baubles eased him. His gaze returned to the large fire opal he'd spotted the first time Allaite showed him the room.

He stood in front of it and became lost in the flickers of light flaring in the gem. This opal was far bigger than the one resting in the high councillor's medallion. A fine sheen of sweat broke out on Rue's brow. It felt as if he were falling into the opal and burning up inside.

"It's beautiful, isn't it?"

The sudden sound of Zalaigh's voice broke whatever spell Rue was under and he jerked around to see Zalaigh standing inside the vault's door.

"What are you doing up?" Rue brushed a shaking hand over his face.

"Same as you. Worrying. I can't help thinking I'm missing something important. Some vital piece of the puzzle." Zalaigh walked over to where Rue stood. They stared at the stone together. "It's just out of my reach, floating there like a star. There's something about his blood. The formula has bonded with it and is slowly solidifying it."

"We know this. You've pointed it out to me. All we seem to be doing is destroying whatever chance his body has to heal itself." Rue slammed his hand on the pedestal holding the opal. "I regret thinking up this foolish experiment. I should have sold the Heart and taken Vlatko on the ride of his life."

Light flooded the room, bathing everything in blood-red. Heat raced up Rue's arm and overwhelmed every atom in his body. He tried to pull his hand away from the pedestal, but some force held it there. The fire shot though his flesh, burning him to a crisp. He threw his head back to scream with the pain and fire blossomed from his mouth.

Rue didn't know how long he stayed fused to the stone, but finally something slammed into him, taking him to the floor and breaking the hold on him. He landed on a hard chest that broke his fall, but no bones. He raised his head enough to stare down at his hands. He expected to see them burnt black with no flesh left on them. He looked up and Zalaigh stared at him. He realised it was Zalaigh he was lying on.

"What the fuck happened?"

Rue suddenly flew through the air again. He closed his eyes, his mind spinning. He came to rest against another hard chest, but the warmth coming off it was familiar. Vlatko ran his hands over his humming body.

"He got mad while he was touching the fire opal. Whatever power lives in him must have boiled over and flashed through him." Zalaigh accepted Allaite's hand to help him up. "Why are you here?"

"I heard him scream." Vlatko shook him slightly. "Rue, open your eyes."

"I will when you stop shaking me. My head is spinning so much, if I open my eyes, I might throw up on you." The violent movement stopped and he opened his eyes to see Vlatko staring down at him with concern. Vlatko's dark eyes widened, causing Rue to wonder what he saw in his gaze.

"Heard him scream? But there wasn't any noise whatsoever." Zalaigh frowned and turned to Allaite. "What are you doing here? Did you hear something?"

"I didn't hear Rue scream, but the entire building shook as if a bomb had gone off somewhere. The shockwave felt like it originated here, so I headed here. I got to the door at the same time as Vlatko." Allaite shot a quick glance at Rue then focused back at Zalaigh. "What happened?"

"Like I said, he got mad and struck the table the opal was on. Next thing I know, he's lit up as bright as a star, fire pouring out of him in every direction. Though it didn't burn anything." Zalaigh sounded puzzled.

Rue leaned against Vlatko. He assessed how he felt. There was lightness to his body as if the fire had burned all the extraneous burdens out of him and all that was left was this power. He'd only felt this strange magic once before—when the firebird had touched him back on the other planet. His back tingled where his birthmark was. Did what had just happened have anything to do with the strange mark? Weakness rushed through his limbs, but he vibrated as well.

"Does this have anything to do with the firebird we interacted with on my planet?" Vlatko's hands shook while he stroked Rue's back.

"Yes, but none of us are ready to discuss it." Zalaigh gestured towards the vault door. "Let's go back to our rooms and rest for a while. In two hours' time, we'll meet up in my study and I'll tell you what you need to know."

The foursome parted company in the hallway, the couples going to their separate rooms. Rue found he supported Vlatko as much as the big man supported him. He chuckled weakly.

"What a pair. Neither one of us would be able to do anything should something bad happen."

"Bite your tongue. Don't tempt fate. Let's get to bed before both of us fall face first onto the floor." Vlatko muscled them into their room and onto the bed.

"That sounds like a wonderful idea." Rue snuggled in tight to Vlatko's chest, avoiding the bandage covering Vlatko's chemo line.

* * * *

Two hours later

Vlatko couldn't take his eyes off Rue. The thief had been pretty before, but after the purging flames of the fire opal, his lover was beautiful. Rue's blond hair touched his shoulders and whenever he moved, little orange sparks flared within the curls. Rue's eyes gleamed as if created from the brightest amber. A fire burned under the surface of Rue's pale skin, making it glow like ethereal alabaster. Vlatko didn't want to touch the thief for fear of marring or soiling Rue's purity.

It wasn't just Rue's looks that had changed. Whenever Vlatko touched him, shocks ran through the assassin's body, giving him a chronic hard-on. He'd always been turned on by Rue before, but this was different. He couldn't get his mind to wrap around any other thought except to bend Rue over the desk in front of them and ream his ass until the thief screamed. Vlatko tried to keep his hands to himself. He feared what might happen if he didn't, but Rue wouldn't let him back off.

Vlatko sat down in the leather chair Zalaigh gestured at, hoping Rue would choose the matching one next to him. Instead, Rue sprawled across Vlatko's lap, pressing his firm ass tight against Vlatko's aching erection. The thief wiggled, trying to get comfortable, but only succeeding in making Vlatko's blood leave his head in a rush, all heading straight for his groin.

"Stop it," he ordered.

"What?" Rue gave him an innocent, wide-eyed look.

"You know." Vlatko grasped Rue's slender hips and rocked his cock along the seam of Rue's pants.

Rue's eyes went hazy as desire caused his skin to flush. "Yeah, I know. Ever since this morning, I've been walking around with a never-ending boner. It gets worse when I get close to you. It's starting to hurt."

Vlatko ignored the other males in the room. He slipped his hand around to cup Rue's cock through his pants. Rubbing his palm over the hard length, he nuzzled the sensitive skin behind Rue's ear. Rue's hips arched up.

"Oh."

Blond curls cascaded over Vlatko's shoulder as Rue shifted to give him more skin to taste. He whispered in Rue's ear, "I can make you come right here. Do you want that? Do you want me to jerk you off in front of them? Does knowing they're watching turn you on?" He circled his palm, applying more pressure. "Or would you rather wait until I can get you back to our room where I can fuck your sweet ass until you scream my name?"

"Please." The moan issued from Rue's throat strangled the word.

"Please what? You have to tell me exactly." Vlatko didn't look up, but he could tell both Allaite and Zalaigh were watching them.

"Later. I want to feel you take my ass. I want you to fuck me so deep I can taste your cum." Rue's words only served to excite Vlatko.

He took his hand off Rue's groin and turned the thief, taking his plump lips with a vicious kiss. Rue gripped his braids, mashing their mouths together until Vlatko felt his lip split. He forced their bodies apart and licked his blood off Rue. A whimper came from the man wound around him, begging him to continue the kiss.

"Not now, love." He cupped the back of Rue's head, pressing the man's face into the nook created by Vlatko's neck and shoulder meeting. He met the amused gazes of Zalaigh and Allaite. "Sorry. I guess the fire's gotten hotter since yesterday."

"Since this morning," Zalaigh corrected. "It's part of Rue's power."

"Power? What do you mean?" Vlatko threaded his fingers through Rue's soft curls. "We have to have sex for the power to work?"

Zalaigh laughed. "No, his power isn't tied to sex. It's just a way for him to burn off the excess power. Once he learns to control it, there will be other ways to deal with it."

Rue sighed, but didn't lift his head off Vlatko's shoulder. Rue stroked along Vlatko's side. He could tell where Rue had touched by the tingle from the fire.

"Rue, turn and look at us. I won't talk about you as if you're not here. This is about your future and your past." Zalaigh poured out four glasses of Mitcovian ale. He gestured for them to follow him. He settled in a chair and Allaite sat down on the floor in front of him. Vlatko carried Rue over and they sat down, but Rue stayed on his lap.

"Rue, do you know who your father was?" Zalaigh absent-mindedly traced his hand over Allaite's skull absent-mindedly as he studied them.

Rue stiffened and Vlatko entwined their fingers, reminding the thief he wasn't alone. "No. My mom never said a word about who he was. She just said she rued the day she met him. Thus my name."

"Did she say anything about him at all?" Zalaigh seemed oblivious to Rue's discomfort.

"She didn't have time to talk to me about him. My mom dumped me on the street, and I don't remember anything she might have said in passing about him. I didn't really have time after that to go looking for him." Rue shot a glance at Vlatko.

Vlatko wondered if Rue worried about what he thought. Vlatko didn't care where Rue came from or what kind of upbringing he'd had. He had no room to judge, since he'd been raised to be a killer.

"It must have been a one-night stand, which doesn't surprise me," Allaite commented.

"I believe your father was a firebird."

Vlatko nodded. He wasn't surprised.

"A firebird? You're fucking kidding me, right?" Rue shot to his feet, pacing in front of them. "There's only one left."

"Firebirds still exist, but they are extremely rare." Zalaigh stood and went to pull a book off a shelf. After flipping through the pages, he found what he was looking for and handed it to Rue.

Rue stared down at a picture of the lady he'd seen in the clearing. Beside her stood a man wreathed in flames, tall and slender with flame-coloured hair. He gave the book to Vlatko and glared at Zalaigh. "Where did they come from?"

Zalaigh shrugged. "No one really knows. They fell from the stars one day on several different planets. None of the legends speak of what galaxy they might have come from. Just that the strange beings arrived in a shower of fire and they have special powers."

Vlatko reached out and touched his hand. "He looks like you do now."

"What do you mean, he looks like me *now*?" Rue's hand shot to his hair. "What the hell do I look like?"

He glanced quickly around the room, looking for a mirror. All he could think of was that somehow the fire had scarred him. Vlatko grabbed his hand and tugged him down to sit next to him.

"Stop it. You were pretty before. Now you're fucking gorgeous." Vlatko kissed him hard.

Unsure if he should believe his lover or not, since he figured Vlatko was a little biased in his favour, he shot a questioning look at Zalaigh and Allaite. Both Mitcovians nodded.

"Vlatko's going to have to be careful when you go out or you'll have people all over you." Allaite's gaze was appreciative.

Vlatko growled under his breath, making all of them laugh. The presence of Vlatko's body next to his settled him down and made him focus better. Rue gestured to Zalaigh. "So tell me why you think my father is or was a firebird?"

"You were describing the way your hands are warm when they touch Vlatko. The heat from them is what has helped ease his pain. When you're angry or caught up in some strong emotion, your eyes turn orange. The firebird appeared to you in her human form. The biggest clue is the birthmark on your back.

I've met a few other offspring of firebirds and they all bear the mark somewhere on their body." Zalaigh nodded towards him.

Vlatko frowned. "How do you know so much about the firebirds?"

"They're a hobby of mine, as are the aliens who were my ancestors." Zalaigh took the book and flipped through the pages, searching for the drawings of the creatures that had flown to his planet. "They had an affinity with water instead of fire, but they were as unusual."

He handed the book to Rue, pointing to the being on the page. Rue leaned against Vlatko and let him look over his shoulder. The artist was so talented, he thought. The creature was tall like Zalaigh, with iridescent blue skin that gleamed as if he wore scales. Where the firebirds burned, this creature flowed like water on the page. Rue ran his finger over the man's picture, feeling as if he could smell the freshness of the liquid.

"They fell from a different part of the universe from the firebirds, but they were much alike." Sighing, Zalaigh stood and walked to the window before looking out. "Where my ancestors successfully colonised this planet and were able to thrive, the firebirds were not. Female firebirds were in short supply, so they began to breed with the native species of the planets they landed on. Their powers got diluted and true firebirds became rare."

Rue slid his hand into Vlatko's. He needed to feel connected to someone. Zalaigh's tale sounded weird and he wasn't sure he believed him. "So my father was a firebird?"

"More than likely. The power transfers from male to male. They don't take care of their young. They breed and then leave, letting the woman they've bred with deal with the child. Your father didn't choose well."

"Well, there's an understatement if I've ever heard one. I shudder to think of what might have happened if my mother had kept me. I've made peace with the fact that my mother was a bitch and she didn't care for me one bit." Rue turned to look at Vlatko. "I've figured out caring for someone isn't necessarily in the blood. It has more to do with needing them and knowing you would give everything you own for them."

Vlatko squeezed his hand. Rue knew his lover understood what he was saying without him having to say the exact words. He wasn't sure if he could, even though he was pretty sure how he felt about the assassin.

"True. The reaction of the fire opal in the treasure room to your power has given me an idea. I think we might have a way of saving Vlatko, but it would require trust from both of you." Zalaigh turned back to look at them.

Vlatko shrugged. "It seems to me I've trusted both you and Rue with my life so far. I'm not about to stop now."

Rue thought about what Zalaigh had done so far for Vlatko and wasn't sure he wanted to subject him to more of that kind of treatment. "Will this be as harsh as the chemo and radiation?"

Zalaigh shook his head. "No. It's a one-time deal. If this plan doesn't work, then there's nothing I can do to help."

Rue shot the Mitcovian a glare and Zalaigh lifted his hands in a helpless gesture. "I have to admit defeat, Rue. Nothing I've done has made any difference and all it's done is make him sicker. Finding a solution to his illness no longer matters. All that matters is his having a good life for what's left of it."

Vlatko turned Rue to look at him. "We've come this far, love. Let's take the ride to the end of the track. We'll figure out what to do after this last shot."

Rue nodded. "You haven't deliberately misled us yet, Zalaigh. Risking it all on one last shot is just the gamble I'd usually play."

Vlatko had already decided to stop the treatments before Zalaigh had told them about this other last ditch effort. He knew they weren't working and they were only making him miss out on the best part of what time he had left. He didn't want to be sick. Vlatko wanted to fuck Rue, and even just spend time with the thief.

Worry coloured Rue's pretty amber eyes, but he smiled at Vlatko. He winked back and turned to Zalaigh. "Let's do this."

Zalaigh nodded. "Allaite, bring the fire opal from the treasure room to the councillor's room."

The security officer frowned. "You're kidding, right?"

Zalaigh shook his head. "No. Bring it. The Councillor's Heart is too small for what we need it to do."

"What do you need it for exactly?" Vlatko pulled Rue to his feet and they followed Zalaigh down the hall.

"The problem we've been having is the way the body armour keeps thickening your blood, causing it to clot. I've seen it under the microscope. Your blood cells have been mutated not only by the formula, but by the genetic enhancements the IUM did to you while you were in the womb. Also, I'm sure they gave you upgrades along the way." Zalaigh smirked at him.

"Sort of like a robot or a computer." Vlatko nudged Rue who gave him a weak smile. He slipped his arm around his slender waist and whispered, "Try not to worry too much. It'll work out in the end."

"What if it doesn't? What if this crazy plan doesn't work and you die?" Rue pulled him to a stop and stared up at him. "I don't want to go back to my old life, Vlatko. I don't want to be lonely again."

Vlatko saw tears well up in Rue's beautiful eyes and love built like a gentle wave in his heart. He embraced Rue, cradling him close to his chest. Vlatko pressed a kiss to Rue's trembling lips. "You won't be alone, love. Zalaigh and Allaite will be here for you and I'm sure somewhere you'll find someone else to take my place."

Rue punched him hard in the chest. Vlatko grunted at the unexpected violence.

"What the hell was that for?"

"I don't want anyone else to take your place, asshole. I want you to stick around for hundreds of years, or at least until I die first." After reaching up, Rue grabbed his head and crushed their lips together.

Vlatko could feel all the emotions Rue couldn't put into words in that kiss. A stray thought raced through his mind. Would Rue ever be able to say the words? Did it really matter if Vlatko never heard them? Did Rue not saying them make the thief's feelings any less true?

The sound of a throat clearing broke them apart. Vlatko turned to see Zalaigh had stopped a few doors down from his suite. They moved, joining him in front of the door. Vlatko saw understanding in Zalaigh's blue eyes.

"Come in. Only one other person has seen this room during my tenure as high councillor. The power of the Heart is concentrated in here. The rituals of binding take place in this room." Zalaigh stepped in.

The lights flared bright and the fire opal in the middle of the medallion the Mitcovian wore refracted the rays back. The blinding beams dimmed to the softness of candlelight. Vlatko looked around the room, searching for a second exit. There wasn't any, and a hint of fear flowed through him. He tended to get claustrophobic when there was only one way out.

The walls were painted an unusual combination of red and blue, almost as if they were mixing fire and water together. The decorations swirled and burst in odd patterns on the ceiling and wall. The floor beneath his feet was smooth Kalsusian marble, which could only be carved and placed by hand. A low altar stood in the centre of the room. It had been etched out of one single chunk of Venuvian crystal.

Vlatko moved closer to it. The legs were decorated with elaborate swirls and designs, very detailed and covering the entire surface. Symbols were etched onto the top of the large middle stone, making up the platform for the altar. Vlatko couldn't read them, but he assumed they were an ancient language. He pointed to them.

"What does it say?"

Rue stood beside him, staring down at the only piece of furniture in the space. If one would even call it furniture. "Is it your language?"

Zalaigh touched a circular symbol on the wall, opening a hidden closet. "It's what our language used to be." He pulled out two robes, one of orange and one of blue. He handed them to Vlatko and Rue. "Here, take off your clothes and put these on."

Rue started stripping without question. Vlatko frowned. He didn't like being without any weapons and, if he was naked, the only thing he could use to protect Rue with was his body. His muscle weakness made him doubt his ability to help if something should happen to the thief.

"Allaite will be here to keep us all safe, Vlatko. Please, put the robe on." Zalaigh pulled out a bowl and a slender knife. The black blade gleamed dully in the light.

Sighing, Vlatko did as he was told. He folded his and Rue's clothes into a neat pile in the corner of the room then put on the blue robe. There must have been magic in the fabric, because it shrank to cover his entire body without ripping. Rue's orange robe did the same.

Rue took his hand and they turned to face the Mitcovian. Zalaigh had stripped as well, but he hadn't put anything else on. He stood before them naked, except for the medallion hanging around his neck and resting in the middle of his chest. The Heart pulsed and Vlatko realised his own heartbeat had calmed to the gem's rate. He casually placed his finger on Rue's wrist where the vein ran to check Rue's heart rate. It matched his.

Power built in the room. Vlatko could feel the pressure weighing on him. The high councillor began to glow, bright blue like water under the noonday sun. Soon Zalaigh was so bright Vlatko couldn't look directly at him. Turning his head, he realised Rue was glowing as well. Only Rue shone a bright gold like the very sun itself.

"Close your eyes, Vlatko. We will guide you to where you need to be." Zalaigh's voice sounded as if it was echoing down a long canyon.

Vlatko didn't argue. There was no point in wasting his breath on words. He'd figured out there was no going back, now that the ritual had got started. Two hands took his. Rue's was the warm one, bathing his hand in heat and easing the ache in his fingers. The other hand was cool, soothing in its own way, as if Vlatko had stuck his hand into tepid bath water. He gave up control, his heart knowing neither man would hurt him deliberately.

Tenderness swamped Rue when Vlatko offered his body up without questioning. There was no hesitation in his steps as he allowed Rue and Zalaigh to lead him towards the altar. Rue shot Zalaigh an uneasy glance. Zalaigh gave him a reassuring smile.

"Don't worry, Rue. We aren't going to sacrifice him. Though there will be a little blood at first." Zalaigh looked over his shoulder. "Ah, Allaite is here now. We can begin."

Rue glimpsed the security officer standing just inside the door, holding the large fire opal in his hands. Allaite's eyes were lowered as if he couldn't bear to look at them. The opal seemed as if it were lit from within. He couldn't take his eyes off it.

"Don't look at it, Rue, or we'll never get the rest of the ritual done. You've already bonded with the gem earlier in the treasure room. When you were engulfed in the fire, it cleansed you of your old being. You'll remember what you've done and all of that, but they'll be faded like distant memories. Now the firebird inside you is reborn. We are going to bond Vlatko to you and to the fire opal." Zalaigh guided Vlatko to the altar, applying some pressure to get the assassin to sit. "Before you lie down, Vlatko, I must make a small cut in your wrist. I'll be making a similar one in Rue's wrist. I need several drops of your blood to mix in the bowl."

"You're not going to bind our wrists together in some primitive covenant ceremony, are you?" Rue laughed shakily. "I'm not going to have to wear that lump around my neck, am I?" He nodded towards the stone Allaite held.

Zalaigh chuckled. "No to both questions. The blood is going to serve as a conduit between the two of you. The fire opal will stay in the treasure room. You'll need to bond with it once a year, renewing the hold it has on you."

"What if I don't?" Rue tried to ignore the sharp black blade coming closer to his wrist.

"You'll get weak and slowly begin to fade away, like I was doing when you brought the Heart back to me. Once you bind with it, Rue, you have no choice. Unfortunately it happened to you before I could explain the consequences."

Rue hissed as the blade sliced through his skin. "Will Vlatko have to renew as well?" He turned to study his lover instead of watching Zalaigh gather his blood in the bowl.

"No. His bonding will happen every time you have sex. It's the emotions created by your joining that will strengthen the bond." Zalaigh ran a finger over the wound and it closed without leaving any mark.

"Our bond should be the fucking strongest one you've ever seen, since we can't seem to keep our hands off each other," he teased, biting his lip as the knife split Vlatko's skin and red blood welled in the wound. "How is it the knife can cut through his skin?"

"The chemo has changed the composition of the body armour slightly. It just wasn't doing enough and I couldn't increase the dosage without truly killing him. I didn't think any of us wanted that." Again, Zalaigh trailed a finger over the wound and it sealed on its own.

Vlatko didn't wince and Rue wondered if he was still awake. He poked the broad shoulder closest to him. "Are you still awake?"

Vlatko grunted. "Yeah, I am, but I didn't think you needed me in the conversation."

"He's right. You are the one who will make this work. He doesn't have to do anything except lie there and be open to whatever you do to him."

"We're going to have sex in front of you, aren't we? I knew you two were voyeurs." The joking tumbled out of his mouth because he was nervous. His power would be the one to heal Vlatko. Power he hadn't known he had until he'd hit that stupid gem.

"No, but if you ever feel the urge to do so, we won't complain." Zalaigh tapped his hand, the touch calming him. "The power inside you will take over once this ritual starts. It will rely on the genetic memories coded into your DNA. Now go and stand at the end of the altar where Vlatko's head is."

Zalaigh used the tip of the dagger to stir the blood in the bowl, mixing it together. He dipped a fingertip in it, reaching out to paint a cross-shaped symbol on Vlatko's forehead. Rue watched with trepidation as Zalaigh walked towards him with blood dripping off his finger. He swallowed back the bile trying to make a quick exit from his stomach.

Breathe, a voice ordered him in his mind.

He took a deep breath, filling his lungs with warm, moist air. He closed his eyes, clenching his hands into fists to keep from grabbing Zalaigh's hand and stopping the Mitcovian.

Something wet traced over his forehead and he managed to convince himself it wasn't blood actually, just red paint Zalaigh had put in the bowl instead.

You'll get through this. If for no other reason than to save Vlatko's life. He deserves your best. The voice sounded suspiciously like the firebird's. He prised his eyes open and searched the room, wondering where she was.

I'm with you in spirit, Rue. Unlike the males of my species, I cannot leave my home. Open yourself to the power inside you. It is what you should be.

Her words weren't for encouragement. They were simply stating the facts as she knew them. He sighed. She was right, though. He'd do it for Vlatko, even if he found himself chained to some large red rock for the rest of his life.

"Vlatko, roll over on your stomach. We need to have access to the spot where the body armour was injected." Zalaigh helped Vlatko move. When the big man was arranged the way the high councillor wanted, Zalaigh waved to Allaite. "Allaite, rest the fire opal right here." He pointed to the spot below Vlatko's right shoulder.

Chapter Sixteen

Vlatko hissed as the weight of the stone was eased onto his shoulder. Pain welled through him and he clenched the sides of the altar to keep from pushing Allaite away. He'd stopped sleeping on his back because of the pressure his own body put on that spot.

"I know the pain is excruciating, Vlatko, but try to clear your mind. If it helps, focus on Rue. What you like about him. What he does that turns you on. Anything to keep from giving the agony the upper hand in your mind." Zalaigh's voice broke through the torment.

Vlatko could do that. An image of Rue lying on their bed evolved in his mind. Those long legs were spread out, giving him an unimpeded view of that slender pretty cock and the pink entrance to Rue's body. Vlatko could taste the saltiness of Rue's sweat as he licked it off Rue's back. The golden glowing skin covering lean muscles enticed him to run his hands over it and through Rue's blond curls.

"Now while he's thinking those things, Rue, put your hands on the opal. Don't press down or you might do more damage than we can fix to Vlatko's back." Zalaigh's instructions were only a background to the moans Rue was making in Vlatko's memories.

A little more weight came to bear on his body and he grunted. It didn't hurt. It was uncomfortable.

"You've always felt the fire inside you, only you've never had the knowledge to use it. That's why your touch eases his pain. Start gathering the power and funnel it through your hands into Vlatko's body. Use the fire opal to amplify the strength. You need to make sure it goes into every inch of his body. You're going to use the fire to liquefy it."

Vlatko tensed. He didn't like the sound of that. A cool hand touched his.

"It's going to hurt, but the firebird has already marked you, so the power should focus on the things that shouldn't be there. It might mean the body armour will no longer be there. We're not sure about that." Zalaigh spoke right next to his ear.

He managed to nod. His forehead brushed the robe Rue wore and he kept it there. It was another connection to the man he loved. A roaring sound burst in his ears and fire burned through him, entering by way of his shoulder. Vlatko wanted to scream, but somehow he understood it would destroy Rue's concentration and that could make things worse for him. Heat raced through his body, following the paths his blood took.

"That's it, Rue, but you need to use more. Vlatko can take it."

Vlatko wasn't too sure about that. His skin felt as if it were going to split from the fire pouring into him. He closed his eyes when the fabric before him began to shimmer like heatwaves. Soon his brain was overwhelmed and he shut down. He couldn't think beyond wanting the pain to stop.

It will. Just a few seconds longer, friend, and you'll be reborn into a healthy body. The firebird's voice rose above the roar of the flames he felt licking along his bones.

Then this will work?

I assume so. It's never been done before to my knowledge, but there is no creature more powerful than a male firebird. The odds are good this will succeed.

He growled. She couldn't have given him platitudes and told him everything was going to be fine? Then, in an instant, the fire was gone, like it had been put out by a strong cold breeze. The weight on his shoulder disappeared and he sat up. There was no weakness or exhaustion. Vlatko felt energised as if he'd taken a long nap.

A lean body hit him in the side. He turned to bring Rue completely into his arms and across his lap. Rue ran his quick, slender hands over his arms and shoulders, up over his face and down around his waist. He knew Rue was reassuring himself that Vlatko was okay. He wanted to tell Rue he was fine, but figured the thief wouldn't believe it until he'd made sure.

Vlatko rested his head on Rue's curls, letting Rue touch him everywhere. When Rue embraced him and the plump lips he loved most in the world pressed hard against his, he knew Rue had calmed down a little. He cupped Rue's firm ass and lifted the thief, helping Rue straddle his thighs.

"Not here. Go back to your suite. We will see you sometime tomorrow." Zalaigh's laughter-filled voice broke into the sexual haze surrounding Rue and

Vlatko. Allaite tossed their clothes on the altar next to them.

"How will we know if this worked?" Vlatko asked without taking his gaze from Rue's amber eyes. He set Rue down and got them both dressed.

"I'll test your blood tomorrow and we'll see." Zalaigh's large blue hand appeared in his line of sight and he stroked it down Rue's back. "Rue's running on adrenaline right now — go have sex and fuck like those long-eared furry creatures humans used to be so fond of. Afterwards, he'll level out and you can get some sleep."

"Yes, sir."

He rose to his feet, picking Rue up again. Rue wrapped his legs around Vlatko's waist, moving his arms to Vlatko's neck. Vlatko broke their visual connection to make sure they didn't run into any walls while making his way to their suite. Rue nibbled along his jaw and down his neck, sucking on sensitive spots as he came to them.

"Fuck." He jumped when sharp teeth bit his earlobe. "If you're not careful, love, I'll fuck you here in the hallway."

Rue rocked his hips against Vlatko's and moaned. "I don't care."

"You might not, but Zalaigh might get upset with us giving his staff a show."

"He's a spoilsport." Rue gave him a little pout.

"It sets a bad example for the servants. Can't have the guests screwing in the halls, it might give them the wrong idea." Vlatko moved into an alcove, pressing Rue's back against the wall. He tugged the curtains closed behind them, so none of the people walking down the hall could see them. "If you want me to fuck you here, you have to be quiet."

He ground their groins together, making Rue push back and tighten his legs around his waist. "Stand up."

Rue frowned, but put his feet on the floor. He squeaked when Vlatko whirled him around and set his hands on the wall. His head fell forward as Vlatko brushed his hair out of the way and bit his neck.

"Remember, you have to be quiet," Vlatko warned as he tore open Rue's pants.

"Quiet. Right, got it," he muttered, not really paying any attention to Vlatko's words. At the moment all he wanted was the big man's hands on his cock and Vlatko's length in his ass.

His pants were pulled down around his ankles. Vlatko pressed one finger on his lips, forcing his mouth open and he sucked it in. Rue heard fumbling behind him, then felt the slap of Vlatko's cock on his ass.

"Get it good and wet. I'm not taking a lot of time to get you ready." His lover fisted Rue's cock, pumping hard and fast.

"Mmm..." There wasn't a connection from his brain to his tongue. All he could think about was the way Vlatko swirled his palm over the head of Rue's cock, spreading his pre-cum up and down his shaft.

Rue sucked and licked, getting Vlatko's finger as wet as possible. His cock slid through his lover's hand and, even with the pre-cum, the friction was rough and Vlatko's grip was tight. His climax began to ripple down his spine and his balls drew tight.

He pulled his mouth from Vlatko's finger and groaned, "Close."

Vlatko's strokes sped up, causing Rue to rock harder between his hand and Vlatko's body. The blunt head of Vlatko's cock bumped against Rue's hole. He wished Vlatko would take him without worrying about hurting him, but Rue knew, even in the throes of passion, Vlatko wouldn't do it.

"Now," Vlatko commanded, biting Rue's shoulder hard enough to break the skin. Vlatko thrust his thick finger deep inside Rue's ass.

Rue turned his head, burying his face against his arm, and stifled his cry. His cum sprayed from his cock, coating Vlatko's hand, Rue's stomach and the wall in front of him. Vlatko kept pegging his prostate, ensuring the thief's climax thoroughly drained him.

When it felt like Vlatko had pumped all of his spunk from him, he rested his head against the wall, his legs shaking. He whimpered when Vlatko's finger disappeared.

"Thanks for providing me with your own personal lube, love." Vlatko's lips brushed over the side of Rue's neck.

Vlatko must have coated his own cock with Rue's cum. Rue bit his lip to keep from crying out as Vlatko eased his shaft into Rue's inner passage. Vlatko had stretched him enough so the pain wasn't overwhelming. He relaxed and pushed back, taking Vlatko deeper.

"This is going to be fast and hard. I'm about to explode," Vlatko warned him after he was buried balls-deep in Rue.

"Take what you need." Rue wasn't going to deny Vlatko anything.

He braced his palms against the wall and spread his legs as far apart as he could get them. Rue rolled his hips, enticing Vlatko to fuck him. Vlatko gripped his waist with both hands and the assassin started reaming his ass. Hard and fast was right. Vlatko pounded his ass, never allowing his cock to slide completely out of Rue.

Rue muffled a scream with his arm again as Vlatko nailed his gland, and kept nailing it. His cock stiffened. After the strength of his last orgasm, he hadn't thought he'd be ready for another so soon. Yet here his body was, ready and able to blow in a few more thrusts. His erection was so hard it ached.

"Now, Rue. I want to feel you come on my cock." Vlatko peeled one hand off Rue's hip, reached around and squeezed Rue's cock.

"Shit," Rue cried out, forgetting to be quiet. His ass clamped down on Vlatko, the big man grunting from the unexpected pressure.

A flood of moist heat bathed his channel as he exploded all over Vlatko's hand a second time. He had enough functioning brain cells left to work his ass, doing his best to make sure Vlatko spilled every last drop of his cum.

Rue slumped forward, managing not to smash face first into the wall. Vlatko's sweat-soaked T-shirt clung to his back when Vlatko leaned on him. Every once in a while his butt would spasm and Vlatko would jerk, but neither of them was truly interested in another round at the moment. Vlatko kissed his shoulder where the bite mark bruised his skin.

The curtain rustled and Vlatko pulled out, turning to face whatever danger might be appearing.

"Are you done frightening the staff yet?" Allaite's amused voice drifted in from the other side of the curtain. "Would you be so kind as to continue this in your rooms?"

"Yeah. We'll head there now." Vlatko looked over his shoulder at Rue and winked. "Rue just couldn't keep his hands off me."

Allaite snorted. "Don't try to pin the whole thing on the thief. I know you were a willing participant. I'll see you both tomorrow." Allaite's footsteps faded away.

Vlatko tugged off his shirt and cleaned them up, along with the wall. Then Rue found himself tossed over Vlatko's shoulder and carried the rest of the way to their suite.

He blinked, trying to keep his eyes open, but the sex must have used up the rest of his adrenaline. Now he wanted to snuggle in Vlatko's arms and sleep for several hours.

Vlatko kept up a soothing caress over Rue's ass and thighs, letting Rue know he was safe and loved. Rue hardly registered being stripped, cleaned up and tucked into bed. What he did notice was when Vlatko slipped under the covers with him and that warm body eased him.

* * * *

Vlatko drifted through the smoke, trying to find the voice calling to him. He pushed the fog away as if it were a curtain hanging to block his vision. A frown formed on his forehead. Who was calling him? Why did they sound so afraid? The fog wasn't hurting anything, though it felt oppressively hot. Sweat rolled down his nose to drip from the tip. He raised his hand to wipe it away and stopped when he saw the flames licking at the tips of his fingers.

"What the hell?" He knew he spoke the words aloud, but he didn't hear them.

Vlatko. The voice moved closer, but he still couldn't see who was speaking.

"Who's there?" he tried to call out. His throat closed and his mouth didn't open.

He's burning up. He doesn't get sick.

Burning up? What were they talking about? He wanted to shout to them that he was there, but suddenly it was like a stone had landed on his chest and he gasped. His lungs collapsed. He tried to move his hands to touch his chest. Something or someone held his hands down. He fought, wanting to tell them he couldn't breathe, but no air found its way into his body.

What do you think is wrong with him? A different voice joined the first. He peered through the curtain veiling his eyes, but all he saw was an orange blur and a blue one standing above him.

Don't know. I'll have to run some tests, but we need to cool him down first. If he gets too hot, he could boil his brain.

Yuck. That sounded disgusting. He agreed with the blue voice, cooling him down was the best thing. His skin tingled and felt like there was pressure building up underneath it. It would split apart soon if they didn't do something to relieve it and maybe that would help with his lungs. Something slipped under his head and a wave of blackness swept over his vision. Vlatko was tired and didn't want to worry about fighting whoever it was touching him. He would just have to trust they wouldn't kill him. Then again, if the heat kept up, killing him might be the best thing for him.

* * * *

"Can you open your eyes?"

The voice whispered into Vlatko's ear. He prised his eyes opened and turned his head to see Rue kneeling next to the bed, chin resting on the mattress and a tired look in his eyes.

"Hey, there. How are you feeling?" Rue's amber gaze brightened when Vlatko blinked at him.

Vlatko opened his mouth to tell him he felt like shit, but nothing came out. His throat felt as if someone had shoved burning embers down it. He tried to touch his neck, but his hand wouldn't go farther than his stomach before he ran out of energy.

Footsteps sounded from the other side of the room while Rue stood and turned.

"He's awake. I think he needs something to drink. The fever probably dried him out." Rue gestured to some point out of Vlatko's view.

"Get him a glass." Zalaigh sat on the edge of the bed, staring at Vlatko. "You gave us a scare. I have to admit, I never thought you'd be the one to do it."

He blinked up at Zalaigh, frowning. Questions ran around his mind, but he couldn't get his tongue to move.

"An hour after you and Rue got to bed, you started running a fever. At first, Rue didn't notice because he says you've always been warm. Then you started sweating and thrashing around as if you couldn't breathe. He came and got us. I had Allaite carry you to the lab." Zalaigh moved when Rue returned with a glass of water.

Rue sat next to him. Vlatko tried to push himself up to be able to drink from the glass, but he didn't have any strength to do it. He was as weak as a newborn. Actually, he didn't think he'd ever been this weak. He gave Rue a helpless shrug.

"Allaite, can you help Vlatko sit up? He'll start feeling better once we get some liquid into him." Zalaigh went to the counter where a microscope sat.

The security officer moved into view and leant down from the other side of the bed, wrapping his arm around Vlatko's shoulder. Allaite lifted him enough for Rue to push pillows behind his back. It was the oddest feeling to be the one being taken care of, instead of doing the caring. He nodded his thanks to the Mitcovian after Allaite eased him back on the pillows and stepped away.

"Here. I'll hold the glass, you sip." Rue held the lip of the glass to his mouth and tipped it slightly.

He opened, allowing the water to flow in. When he got enough to rinse his mouth, he tapped Rue's leg. The thief pulled the water away and smiled. Vlatko could tell Rue had been worried and still was. Those amber eyes watched his every move. He swished the water around his mouth, moistening the dry tissue.

Swallowing, he moaned softly. The water felt good going down. He touched Rue's thigh again and the glass was returned to his lips. He gulped more down, emptying it before he'd let Rue take it away.

He licked his lips to wet them. Taking a deep breath, he realised the pressure on his chest was gone. "What was wrong with me?"

Rue touched his chest, stroking gently over his skin. "You had a fever. It got so high, we were afraid it would fry your brain." Fear showed in Rue's gaze. "Zalaigh thinks it might have been some kind of reaction to the ritual we performed yesterday."

Vlatko jerked. "Yesterday! I've been unconscious an entire day?"

Rue nodded, blond curls bouncing. "I was fucking freaked. You could have awoken with scrambled brains or something." A light punch landed on his chest. "Don't ever fucking do that again."

He took Rue's fist in his hand and brought it to his lips, brushing a kiss over the knuckles. "I don't plan on doing it any time soon. At least, not the ritual thing, which is what you assume did this to me, right?" He glanced at Zalaigh.

The Mitcovian nodded. "I took a blood sample during the height of your fever. It looks like your blood cells were kick-started in some way. They've absorbed and transmuted the troublesome atoms. Instead of being seen as a foreign object or substance, your body has written it into its DNA and now accepts it as part of your genetic makeup. You won't be experiencing any more weakness, but won't lose any of the enhancements the IUM created in you."

Vlatko didn't know if he should feel glad. At least he wasn't going to die. He stared at Rue, whose expression mirrored his uncertainty.

"We accomplished what you wanted when you came here. Now that you're going to live for a long time, what are you going to do?" Allaite asked, leaning against the counter next to Zalaigh.

Vlatko shrugged. "I don't know. I guess I never really believed we'd cure me, so I never planned a future."

"Hmmm..." Zalaigh nudged Allaite with his shoulder. "You need to go back to your suite and rest. I think you're out of danger. You're welcome to stay here for as long as you want, even living here is an option."

Vlatko flung the blankets back and stood up. Ignoring the fact that he was naked, he headed towards the door.

"Wait a minute, stud. I can't let you walk down the hall giving everyone a show. My staff will be useless after that." Zalaigh tossed him a sheet.

He wrapped it around his waist then held out his hand for Rue. "You'll come with me, right?"

"No matter what your decision is, I'll follow you." Rue took his hand, smiling at Zalaigh as they left.

"What do you think they'll decide to do?" Allaite rested his chin on Zalaigh's shoulder as they watched the thief and the assassin walk out of the room.

"The only thing that'll keep Rue safe. They'll stay here." Zalaigh pottered around, putting slides and tubes away.

"What makes you think that?" He grabbed Zalaigh, tugging him tight against his body.

Zalaigh looped his arms around Allaite's neck, leaning back slightly to meet his lover's gaze. "Vlatko knows the IUM will hang around, like starving wolves following a wounded deer. They'll wait until they get Rue alone and then they'll move in. The IUM have a long memory and they don't forget people who screw them over."

"So there's safety in numbers?" Allaite licked a line along Zalaigh's chin.

"Mmm...yes. Vlatko hasn't lost any of his abilities, but he knows his objectivity is shot. He'll be worried about Rue too much to keep an impartial eye on him. And the more people keeping an eye on the thief, the safer he'll be." Zalaigh dropped his head back, giving Allaite access to more of his neck.

"Good. I could use Vlatko as one of your personal guards. His training makes him the best choice. He and I have a mutual agreement. We take care of our lovers, individually and together." Allaite nipped Zalaigh's earlobe.

Zalaigh shivered and a smile skated across Allaite's face. "What if your lovers feel they can take care of themselves?"

Allaite pushed Zalaigh back against the counter, forcing him to sit down and spread his legs. He rubbed their groins together, making Zalaigh moan.

"Rue and you can take care of yourselves, but it doesn't hurt to have back-up. Who better to look after your asses than men who have a vested interest in them?" Allaite pressed his hand hard against Zalaigh's cock. "I think I'd like to take a closer look at yours."

Zalaigh groaned, and Allaite proceeded to guard Zalaigh's ass.

* * * *

Rue and Vlatko lay in bed, wrapped around each other. Vlatko ran his hand up and down Rue's back, investigating the bumps of the thief's spine. Rue pressed his lips to Vlatko's rough cheek.

"We did it." He grinned down at Vlatko.

"You did it. All I did was lie there." Vlatko winked.

"It doesn't matter who did what. You're going to live. What are we going to do now?" He frowned, trying to figure out where they would go. He didn't really want to go back to that primitive planet.

"We can stay here. Zalaigh gave us his word we would be welcomed here, no matter what. I'm sure I can get a place on the security detail and we'll find something for you to do. That way you won't get bored. I know you don't need money or anything, but I'm sure Zalaigh could use you as a consultant or something." Vlatko kept his gaze on Rue.

"It sounds like you've got it all figured out." Rue traced a finger down Vlatko's nose. "What do you want to do? Because what I said in the lab was the truth. No matter what you decide, I'll follow you."

He ducked his head to look at Vlatko's chest instead of his eyes. Fear swirled around in his heart, but he knew it was the truth. There wasn't anywhere he wouldn't go as long as Vlatko was with him. The commitment scared him, but he'd realised while Vlatko was sick that he'd already committed himself to the relationship, when he'd chosen to return the Councillor's Heart instead of selling it. When he'd chosen finding a cure for Vlatko over his own life's training.

"First, I'm going to contact Stargazer and have him let Three know we might have figured out a cure. I'm sure Zalaigh can figure something out using heat and lasers. He just needs more time, which our binding with the fire opal has given him. As for us, I think we should stay here. We'll be safe from the IUM here. Also, we'll have people who'll help us watch out for each other all around us. Plus, we have friends here." Vlatko lifted his chin so his lover's dark gaze met his own. "We'll be together and that's all that matters."

Rue nodded and leant down to kiss him. Vlatko cupped his ass, teasing his hole. He moaned and straddled Vlatko's hips. They rocked together, trying to get as close as possible. Vlatko rolled over, putting Rue on his back.

As Vlatko slid deep into Rue's ass, Rue knew they were home for each other. His heart had found the family he hadn't even known he needed. He wrapped his arms around Vlatko's shoulders, encouraging his lover to take him and claim him.

Epilogue

Two months later

Vlatko stood behind Zalaigh's right side, watching him work the room. It was a formal party welcoming the Venuvian ambassador to Mitcov. So far, everything looked good and they weren't expecting any trouble. Laughter drifted over the din of conversation. He turned his gaze towards the hilarity.

Men, some who looked at Rue as a colleague and some who looked at the beautiful blond with lust in their eyes, surrounded his lover. Rue glowed, his skin golden and his amber eyes shining bright. Vlatko glanced around and spotted one of Allaite's guards near Rue, but not making Rue feel hemmed in.

A hand tapped his shoulder. Turning, he saw Allaite standing there.

"I'll take over. You're off duty as of now, so maybe you should go make those men jealous." Allaite nodded towards Rue.

"Thanks." Vlatko grinned and winked at the security officer.

He made his way through the crowd, nodding at strangers and friends alike. He didn't let anyone stop him. As he got closer to the group, he noticed three men circle around his lover. One of them glanced over his shoulder and fear shot through Vlatko. It was an IUM assassin.

He shoved people out of the way. One of the assassins reached for Rue's shoulder.

"Rue, down."

Rue dropped to the floor without questioning. Vlatko was glad he'd worked with the thief on what to do if someone ever came after him. He wrapped his hand around the grip of his laser and drew it as he closed in on the assassins. Allaite and Rellam backed him up. Vlatko saw them surround the other two men. Rue rolled away, clearing the area so Vlatko wouldn't have to worry about his safety.

The first shot was for the man closest to Rue. Vlatko didn't wait to see if the shot had landed. He swung and hit the other guy in the leg. He aimed for the kneecap, one of the most vulnerable parts on a human. By then, he was in close enough to swing his fist holding the gun at the third man's face. The satisfying crunch of the man's nose breaking made Vlatko smile. These weren't his fellow assassins. They weren't enhanced or genetically altered. Three would have told the created assassins the possibility of a cure existed. He hoped they had defected.

All three assassins were down within minutes. Vlatko stood over them, gesturing for the Mitcovian security guards to drag the two living would-be killers out of the room. One of the servants covered the first assassin with a tablecloth. Vlatko's shot had nailed the man in the chest. Regret didn't exist in Vlatko's heart for this man's death. Even though Vlatko had made a promise never to kill again, he would murder anyone if it kept Rue safe.

Tucking his laser away, he turned to find Rue on his feet and in the middle of a crowd. Rue's amber eyes met his and all Vlatko wanted was to hold him, making sure his lover was safe. He slid between the men, wrapping his arm around Rue's waist, then crushed the slender body tight to him. He took Rue's plump lips with authority. Rue entwined his arms around Vlatko's neck and tangled a leg around Vlatko's thigh. The thief yielded without argument and opened to Vlatko.

Vlatko slid his tongue into Rue's mouth, stroking the sensitive skin behind his lip. Rue's sweet moan teased Vlatko's ears. He nibbled then moved along the chin. Rue tipped his head, baring more of his skin to Vlatko's mouth. Cupping the firm little ass, Vlatko lifted him up and started moving towards the exit.

"All the pretty ones are taken," one of the visitors muttered.

Allaite touched his shoulder as he went past. "Take him out of here. We'll talk about this tomorrow."

Vlatko smiled against Rue's lips. After they got into the empty hallway, he dropped Rue, so his lover could stand up. Rue's feet touched the floor and his hands stayed entangled in Vlatko's braids. He pushed the man up against the wall. Their groins rubbed together and both men groaned. Rue's eyes gleamed bright orange and heat radiated from his skin.

Within minutes, they were naked, but a door shutting farther down the hall stopped them. He threw Rue over his shoulder, gathered their clothes and headed down to their suite. In the room, he tossed Rue onto the bed.

"Gods, I love you."

Rue's words surprised and pleased him because Rue rarely said them. Vlatko knew it stemmed from Rue's upbringing, so when Rue lowered his guard to make that statement, the words had to be true.

"Spread," he ordered.

Rue reached behind his knees, lifting his legs up and back. Vlatko's breath caught as Rue's pink pucker was exposed to his gaze. He ran his finger down the vein running along the underside of Rue's cock. He played with the tender bit of skin behind Rue's balls and the slender thief groaned. He slid his fingers down to tease Rue's hole, pushing in a little then pulling out.

"Ready, are you?" Vlatko thrust his finger all the way in and Rue arched off the bed.

Vlatko leant down to give Rue a kiss with teeth and tongue while inserting two fingers into Rue's ass. He spread them, stretching Rue and trying to make sure his lover was loose enough to take him in. Rue moaned and begged.

"Please. Vlatko, I want you in me."

Vlatko thrust into Rue, took Rue's legs over his arms and started to slide into his ass. He pegged Rue's gland, riding him slow and easy. He'd had a hard-on since before the party had started, and realising that Rue had prepared himself earlier turned him on even more. Rue's power burned between them, heating Vlatko's skin until sweat dripped from his forehead. This was the best way to work off the excess fire in Rue. Vlatko enjoyed it.

Rue knew how to work his hips, body and ass, bringing Vlatko to climax quickly. Vlatko felt his balls tighten and pleasure pooled at the base of his spine. He fisted Rue's cock and stroked. He knew Rue liked it when he twisted his hand around the head of Rue's cock. He pressed his thumb into the slit at the tip of

Rue's shaft and Rue cried out, shooting cum all over his lean stomach and Vlatko's hand.

The strength of Rue's muscles clamping down on Vlatko's length drew his climax from him. He growled as he spilt his spunk deep into Rue's ass, renewing the claim he'd made on the beautiful thief.

"I love you, my firebird," he whispered in Rue's ear as he slumped to the side and snuggled Rue tight to him.

About the Author

There is beauty in every kind of love, so why not live a life without boundaries? Experiencing everything the world offers fascinates TA and writing about the things that make each of us unique is how she shares those insights. When not writing, TA's watching movies, reading and living life to the fullest.

T.A. Chase loves to hear from readers. You can find her contact information, website details and author profile page at http://www.totallybound.com.

Totally Bound Publishing